Alfred Leigh

Fetters of Memory

A Novel: Vol. II.

Alfred Leigh

Fetters of Memory
A Novel: Vol. II.

ISBN/EAN: 9783337032388

Printed in Europe, USA, Canada, Australia, Japan

Cover: Foto ©Andreas Hilbeck / pixelio.de

More available books at **www.hansebooks.com**

FETTERS OF MEMORY.

A Novel.

IN TWO VOLUMES.

BY

ALFRED LEIGH.

AUTHOR OF " EL DORADO," " MAUD ATHERTON," &C.

VOL. II.

London :

REMINGTON AND CO.,

New Bond Street, W.

1882.

FETTERS OF MEMORY.

CHAPTER I.

Is it a morbid fancy, or a flash
Of light prophetic, from the years to come,
Which finds its language in the creeping mist,
And stirs mad longings for the vanished days?
In truth I know not clearly—only this—
To-night my heart is sad and comfortless.

IT is curious and not very encouraging to observe
that while the artless grace, instinctive truthful-
ness, and ready affection of childhood soon disap-
pear; the less amiable traits of nursery life cast
a dark shadow—grotesque and exaggerated perhaps, but still an undeniable shadow on a man's
character in later years, until long after his hair
is grey. The outbursts of unreasoning anger, the
idle regret over lost trifles, and the insensibility
to plain reason and common sense, are dignified
by mystifying names, when they appear in people

playing an important part in the social, political,
or theological worlds; but the disguise is merely
transparent, and they are easily recognised as belonging properly to the period of pinafores and
popguns.

Perhaps if Percy Fenwood's character had been
minutely analysed, a good many impulses and
tendencies of this kind would have been discovered; but the most prominent of them all,
was the inconstant affection for new toys. The
necessity of being amused was an important item
in his philosophy; and for any charm to be complete, it was above all things necessary that it
should be new. Some of his friends believed him
incapable of strong affection, and this was partly
true, for he was always occupied in learning the
alphabet of love, thus giving himself no opportunity to explore the boundless worlds of its
literature.

But of all the playthings which had succes-
sively absorbed his attention, none had ever pleased
him half so much as his wife. He liked the respect
and tacit admiration which her beauty everywhere
commanded—it was pleasant to hear her sweet

voice trying to frame some idiomatic phrase, in a language she had hitherto only known through the inanimate medium of lesson-books—to enjoy her unfeigned delight and wonder at the sights over which the ordinary tourist merely yawned; moreover, her companionship altogether, was brightly unlike anything he had ever known before; and he wrote to his friend Morris in London, so glowing an account of married felicity as nearly to induce that susceptible young gentleman to send Miss Kennedy a full avowal of his ardent emotions, and his desire to renounce the unsatisfying pleasures of bachelor existence for ever.

In those days of Continental travel, Alice was not unhappy. All the influence of her life had conduced to develope the practical rather than the imaginative elements of her character; and besides this her clear judgment aided by her strong sense of duty, taught her to accept the inevitable present, and not to fritter away vital energy by needless longing after the unattainable. Percy's affection at this time was constant, considerate, and almost chivalrous: she liked him too well to be indifferent to this, and his solicitous anxiety to anticipate her slightest want, was an experience almost as new to her, as the strange scenes through which they passed.

To most people a tour through France and Italy is rather a wearying and disappointing thing : too much is attempted, and as an inevitable consequence nothing is really done ; and the traveller returns exhausted with only a tangle of memories, in which long dusty roads, crowds chattering in unintelligible tongues — seemingly interminable vistas of coloured canvas, and bewilderingly contrasting church spires pointing to a cloudless sky, mingle together in hopeless confusion.

But to Alice it seemed as though the belief in fairyland, with which she entered Seafern Hall had returned once more. She had never seen a city before, and her conceptions of one were mainly founded on the market-town ten miles from Seafern — her ideas of a church had scarcely soared above the weather-beaten building where Mr. Ellis talked to the fishermen ; and now she found people walking in the midst of stately

cities and ancient cathedrals, apparently unconscious that there was anything remarkable about
them. Most of all perhaps, she was fascinated by
the undreamed-of treasures of art, now for the
first time revealed to her—she knew nothing of
chiaroscuro or tender tints—she had learned none
of the fashionable cant of the studio and its
votaries—she had not even been taught the pictures it was correct to admire. But she had quick
eyes and rapid sensibilities, and if her judgment
was not always in strict accordance with the approved canons of orthodox criticism, it was generally true, and never wholly deceived by mere show
and glitter. A maiden of the pre-Raphaelite
school once smiled disdainfully at her, as she
stood looking with wonder and reverence at a
work of the early Renaissance, and she passed
more than one historical masterpiece, with the
fatal observation—"What a pity it's all faded;"
but the paintings expressed unutterable things to
Alice—she could worship art devoutly, though
none of the great sects of taste had ever conferred
the right of membership upon her—though she
had never subscribed to their dogmatic creeds, or

mastered the intricacies of their accepted liturgies and songs. Sculpture she did not so readily understand, being impressed by it as by a poem written in an imperfectly comprehended language, not that she was insensible to beauty of form, but her heart still beat with too rapid and impatient life to be in perfect sympathy with the passionless repose of marble.

In this manner three months passed by, Alice generally pleading for another week's travel, when Percy suggested that they should return to England. Sometimes they encountered chance acquaintances, to whom he was proud to introduce his young wife, and who generally expressed surprise among themselves, that a country girl could wear her honours so lightly, and could be so little disconcerted by contact with people more deeply versed in the unwritten laws and customs of society.

On the last of these occasions they were accosted by a young man, who left nothing to be desired, so far as the cut of his coat and the curl of his moustache were concerned; and who evinced by the complacent drawl of his conversation, his conviction that these were the most important interests of life; and the other matters earthly or divine which absorbed the thoughts of humanity, merely inevitable and insignificant sequences. Characters of this kind need such careful analysis for the discovery of any individuality, and there are so many things in the world worthier attention, that Alice after a polite recognition almost forgot his presence, when she was startled by the mention of a name that had been oftener in her thoughts recently, than she would have admitted even to herself.

"Have you seen Mayfield lately Fenwood?"

"No, I had no idea he was in this part of the world. Do you know where he is now?"

"In Venice probably—he left here two days ago, I wonder you've not met him in any of your rambles."

That evening when they were alone at dinner together, Percy said rather abruptly—

"Shall we go back to Venice, and see if we can find Mayfield there?"

"No," she answered quickly, "I am beginning to think you are right after all, and that if we travel much longer, our eyes will be wearied with beauty, and we shall lose the appreciation of it altogether."

"I'm delighted you've come to that conclusion, for my own part I'm bored to death with sight seeing. The only beauty I never get tired of is yours Alice."

"You may weary of that some day," she answered only half in jest, "but I won't spoil your compliment by scepticism. To return to the practical question, if you wish to go home, I am ready."

"Well then, let us start the day after to-morrow;" and the arrangements were made accordingly.

They reached London about the end of January and Alice's first impressions of the world's greatest city were not favourable. It has been pithily though rather mercilessly declared, that a fine day in England is like looking up a chimney, and a wet day like looking down one. The hour of their arrival belonged decidedly to the latter class; for there was a heavy fog on the town—the rain was falling in a slow, melancholy, persistent drizzle;

and the snow storm of two days before had with the assistance of miscellaneous traffic, converted the streets into a dreary waste of mud.

"London is not beautiful like Paris," said Alice, after the first disappointing glimpse, and Percy answered—

"No, it may justly lay claim to being a prodigy of ugliness; there's no place like it to live in for all that."

They drove rapidly through the misty streets until they reached a house, large and handsome, but not particularly inviting or cheerful, where the carriage stopped; and Percy gave her his hand to assist her to alight, with the words—

"This is home darling—may it be a very happy one for you. I am famished for my dinner, so I won't let you look over it till we've had something to eat."

As they had not been expected so early however, the dinner could not be ready for at least half-an-hour; so as Alice declined to recognise the plea of fatigue as valid, they went through every room together. She could not but admire what she saw, for nothing that taste and lavish

expenditure could accomplish, had been left
undone.

"You are an extravagant boy," she said after
they had seen everything, "one would fancy you
possessed the eight diamond statues in the old
story."

"I never read it—you shall tell me all about
them some day; at the present moment I think
I could exchange eight hundred statues for a good
dinner—I don't think I ever so fully understood
the character of Esau."

"Never mind Esau—you shall have your mess of
pottage directly. You have not told me how you
like this dress, which you made me buy in Paris."

"It does very well for travelling," he returned,
surveying it critically, "but you must get a better
style of thing for society."

Alice gave a sigh of resignation. "I see very
clearly that I shall ruin you," she said, "you
must have spent a fortune on jewels alone. Those
diamonds you gave me make me nervous every
time I look at them. I wish you would not give
me such expensive things; I have nothing in return
to give you."

"Nonsense Alice, don't you remember how Falstaff said to Prince Henry 'Thou owest me a million pounds—thy love is worth a million—thou owest me thy love.' I'm not sure the quotation is quite right, but that's the effect of it. I never can remember the poets, except when their words are quite irrelevant; the only poetical phrase I can be certain of at this moment is that fine line of Byron's, 'the tocsin of the soul—the dinner bell,' and by Jove there's the reality. Madam may I offer you my arm?"

And with mock ceremony he took her down-stairs.

After dinner was over, and he had sat for some time in lazy enjoyment of walnuts and wine, he glanced at his watch and said—

"Why its only a quarter past eight—there's a fellow not living far from here I want to see to-night. There'll be a lot of things for you to look after; for you won't take my advice and leave these matters to servants, so you'll like to be alone."

Alice looked rather surprised but said nothing; so construing her silence into acquiescence, he

went into the uninviting street, without the idea
that to leave a young wife on their first evening
at home, was scarcely considerate even occurring
to him. His object was to see Henry Drummond,
and avert the possibility of his calling at the
house; for that gentleman's bearing to ladies,
though doubtless insinuating in the highest
degree, was not what Alice was accustomed to;
and her rapid perceptions might read more in the
man's words and manner than it was advisable
she should know. Moreover, the taste for gambling though it had not then grown into a passion,
had been sharpened by his three months' abstin-
ence from it; and he felt strongly inclined for a
game at cards or billiards.

And meanwhile Alice sat alone, amidst the
wealth and luxuries of her new home, with a head
aching from the noise and bustle of the day's
journey, and a heart not free from anxiety and
misgiving. Morbid anticipation was not a habit
with her; but the vague sense of fear surrounded
her, as the mist without crept through the
smallest crevices and entered even the gaily
lighted room. Her will was strong, and she strove

at first to reason it away, and then to banish it from her mind altogether; but her efforts were futile, and at length she murmured to herself—

"It is of no use—I cannot help being sad to-night; and yet everything here is so beautiful, and Percy is always kind. Perhaps it is my nature to be ungrateful and discontented; when I was at Seafern I never half appreciated Mr. Fenwood's goodness, and I cared nothing for the people there, until I knew I was soon to leave them, and yet—and yet "—

She ceased to utter her thoughts aloud, but the colour on her cheeks heightened, and it would have been easy for anyone who knew her story, to see that she was living over again the evening when she had first been perfectly happy—when her heart had throbbed with grateful gladness at the knowledge that the love she cared for most on earth was hers. At last she rose abruptly from her reverie, and said firmly—

"I have forfeited the right to indulge in thoughts like these, and I will not—yet it is hard to know that the sweetest moments God has given me must be hidden out of sight for ever."

CHAPTER II.

I will work him
To an exploit, now ripe in my device
Under the which he shall not choose but fall.

HAMLET.

WHATEVER troubles and disappointments Alice might find in her new home, the weariness of involuntary indolence was not among the number. This was owing entirely to her own firmness, for Percy had wished her to procure the aid of a housekeeper, and virtually ignore domestic detail altogether. "I want you to enjoy yourself," he said, "and not trouble your head about whether the rooms are dusted and the dinner properly cooked." But Alice had so resolutely resisted this proposal, and had urged so many reasons for undertaking the work of management herself, that he had been obliged to let her have her own way. The servants were nearly all from Seafern—they had known Alice since she was a child—they were sincerely attached to her, and although this affection did not prevent some of the younger ones from idleness, blundering, and indiscreet flirtations, it had an undoubted influence upon them, drew a distinct boundary-line between transgressions that might safely be indulged in, and offences that could not be condoned; and lent microphonic assistance to the otherwise inaudible voice of conscience.

Among her duties as mistress of a London house, there were few so little to her taste, as the ordeal of receiving and returning formal calls. Percy had rather a large circle of acquaintances, and for the first few months not a week passed without a party of some kind, either at their own home or at the house of a friend. This of course necessitated further visiting, and Alice at length came with philosophic resignation to regard London life as a kind of purgatory, in which souls were purified not by penal fires, but by conversational platitudes and the interchange of cards.

Among the first people to call upon her were Mrs. Stafford and her daughter Ethel, who were singularly affectionate for relations who had been silent so many years. When Alice heard that her mother's brother was living, her first feeling was

one of resentment as she remembered how he had
slighted his sister long ago; and if she herself
had still been poor, she would probably have been
too proud to respond to their friendly overtures.
As it was however, the longing to hear something
about her fair young mother, and the feeling that
she was too good and gentle to be the cause of
any bitterness, gained the victory; and Alice in-
vited Mr. and Mrs. Stafford with their daughter
to dinner, early in the following week.

"If you are not engaged next Tuesday," she
said, "I hope you will come—I should like you to
see my husband; and we shall be quite alone—
you will probably prefer that to meeting people
you don't know—will you tell Mr. Stafford I shall
be disappointed if he does not join you?"

"She's a ladylike girl," remarked Mrs. Stafford on the way home, "and their furniture is
really splendid. They must be richer than your
papa thought, or else they are very extravagant.
Is Alice (its absurd to call one's niece by anything
but her Christian name) at all like what you expected Ethel?"

"Not much—there's a presence about her I

didn't look for in a country girl; and she is certainly handsome in a striking brilliant way, but I've seen faces I like much better." Ethel was probably thinking of her mirror, and endeavouring to satisfy herself with forcible reasons for her preference; for she was silent a few seconds, and then resumed in a brighter tone—"Yes, it isn't my ideal of beauty—and did you notice her hands?"

"No, what about them?"

"They were not large, I admit that; but they were quite brown, and didn't look soft a bit. I suppose she'd been rowing or something of that sort, and exposing them to the sun. For my part, I think it's a girl's duty to keep her hands soft and white:" and having by this time re-established her self-esteem, which the first glimpse of Alice had momentarily ruffled, Ethel Stafford recovered her wonted serenity.

"You will like my cousin," said Alice that evening to Percy, after she had told him about the morning's visitors; "she is such a pretty girl—I should think she would be just your style."

"Well, what are we to do with her mother?

I'm glad I haven't a troop of relations—it's always difficult to know how to dispose of them. Now, on Tuesday, for instance—you'll want to talk with your uncle—I must make myself agreeable to the fair Miss Ethel, who's to be polite to the mamma? I have it—I'll ask Morris down, to complete the number. If there's any truth in the evolution theory, I think he must be descended from a piece of wadding, he does so admirably for fitting into odd places, and is so useless for any other object."

"A glowing testimony to the worth of a friend truly," said Alice, smiling, "but you are quite right, we must have a sixth at the table, though I said we should be alone; so if you have no scruples in immolating Mr. Morris on the altar of necessity, get him to come by all means."

The device succeeded admirably, for no sooner was Mrs. Stafford introduced to the unoffending bachelor (whose probable ancestry Percy had described in so uncomplimentary a fashion), and observed his glances of furtive admiration at Ethel, than divining by a mysterious instinct that his social position left much from a financial point of view to be desired, she determined to monopolize him herself, and so prevent the possibility of exposing Ethel's susceptibility, to the danger of a *tête-à-tête* conversation—a precaution by the way, which was quite unnecessary, that young lady being perfectly well able to take care of herself.

So Percy found the occasional remarks, which it was his duty as host to offer to each of his guests, scarcely needed in Mrs. Stafford's case; and gladly availed himself of her preoccupation to pay the more marked attention to her daughter, whose pretty face and self-possessed manner had considerable charm for him.

Mr. Stafford's keen eyes had after a rapid scrutiny of Alice, softened into a gentler expression than was habitual to them. "There's character in that girl," he thought—" intelligence, firmness, and endurance : she is wonderfully like poor Grace, but it is easy to see that her sailor father's blood is running in her veins. After all, he was a likely fellow if he hadn't been so poor; and that proud, fearless look suits a handsome woman—it's such a contrast to the simper of

welcome one so often meets in society from women
who would far rather one stayed away;" and
recalling several instances of such greetings with
contemptuous impatience, he sat down to make
himself agreeable.

He did not fail, for Alice was deeply interested
in all he had to tell; and the shrewd man of
business never marred a story by tedious reitera-
tion, or gave offensive prominence to his money-
making ethics; although he might sometimes
show a shallowness of feeling or a blunted power
of perception. On the whole Alice liked him—he
was sensible and amusing when he spoke on indifferent subjects, and not wholly wanting in natural
affection when alluding to his childish home.

After dinner Ethel played and sang charmingly,
Alice thought; and the whole evening was probably very pleasant to all of them except Herbert
Morris, who subsequently declared he had never
been so fatigued in all his life. The intimacy
thus begun did not end here; and it soon became
an understood thing that the Staffords were welcome whenever they cared to come: as a natural
consequence, Ethel conceived a violent affection

for Alice—called on her—walked with her—drove with her—wrote her long letters, and declared she was the sweetest girl in the world.

Although she did not respond to this enthusiastic homage in quite the same strain, Alice liked her cousin, viewed every grace and accomplishment she possessed in the most favourable light, and idealised her—not, it is true, into a heroine—but into the very thing she was not, a warm-hearted, affectionate girl. It is always difficult to shake off the childish notion that selfishness is unlovely in appearance as well as in fact, and associate with a fair face a hard or a shallow heart. Moreover, Ethel's manner favoured illusions of this kind : she was not unamiable, unless thwarted, and kept the angles of her character out of sight with artistic ability. "I am not so rich in friends," Alice thought, "that I should slight this one." Occasionally she called at Clapham, and soon won the hearts of the younger children—Walter however, she did not see, as he was now engaged with his father in the city, and rarely returned home until late in the evening.

"I begin to think your fine prize won't be

worth so much after all," said Ford to Drummond about this time; " your hopeful pupil hardly ever comes now."

" We are changing characters," the other retorted with a smile; " I used to be the impatient man and you the one who could wait—now it's just the other way. I tell you the fish has swallowed the hook; and we should be fools if we didn't let him play with the line till he was tired. I know the boy's character—trust me for that: he can think of nothing but his wife now, but he'll soon get tired of that, as he does of everything except play; and then it will be our turn."

The gambler was right—in a few months a change began in Percy. At first it was so slight that the most watchful eyes could not have detected it; or if they had perceived the fact, they would still have been unable to explain its nature. But Alice at length discovered that her influence over him was weaker than it had been—that he cared less for her society—that he oftener made excuses for being away from home.

There was no actual coldness between them, and anything like that everyday episode—a matrimonial quarrel, there seemed no need for her to fear, as she was unselfishly earnest in her intention to do right, and Percy retained the careless good-nature which had been his characteristic from a child. Still she knew with cruel certainty that the elements of discord were there, and strove by every innocent device that she could think of, to make their attitude towards each other the same as it had been when they were first married.

At first she succeeded, but only for a little while; for Percy was like the Sultan Schahriar in his desire for entertaining novelties; and Alice had not Scheherazade's power of satisfying these somewhat unreasonable demands. She would ask herself sometimes if this was owing to any fault of hers; and her cheeks often flushed with the knowledge that the most potent talisman was always wanting in the spells she strove to weave —the undivided love of a woman's heart.

She had resolved to indulge in no thought of Sydney; but she might as well have forbidden the blood to flow through her veins at every throb of her heart: the remembrance of him was in the air she breathed—in the books she read; and she could no more control her wandering thoughts by day than her mocking dreams by night.

She saw much clearly now that had been dim to her before; she reproached herself for having yielded to the coercion of external circumstances, against the teaching of her own heart, and the dictates of her instinctive convictions. "I deserve to be miserable," she thought; "but must I always be reaping such a bitter harvest?"

Percy saw nothing of all this, and would have laughed at the idea of any important change in himself. "Alice is not such good fun as she used to be" he thought sometimes, but the idea only crossed his mind like a fitful shadow, and never left behind it any permanent feeling of disappointment. The taste for gambling had grown into a habit, so that although he had less belief in Drummond than formerly, he had not sufficient force of resolution to shake him off; but the habit had not yet deepened into a passion, and he was on too good terms with himself to be troubled with any misgivings as to its effect in the future.

There was one person, however, who with far slighter opportunities for observation, but deeper knowledge of the cause, saw the exact state of affairs as clearly as Alice herself. This was Mary Ford, who from time to time watched him enter her father's house with a weary foreknowledge of how all this would end. She had pleaded for strangers of whom she knew nothing, but her sympathy was doubled when she perceived how inexorably the web was closing round Percy, and how hopeless it must soon be for him to escape. His handsome face and the easy courtesy of his manner on the two or three occasions when chance threw her in his way quickened her sympathy, and she looked constantly for the possibility of warning him that craft and treachery were leagued against him—in imploring him never to enter the guilty house again.

For a long time she sought an opportunity in vain, for Drummond almost invariably walked home part of the way with Percy, and her repugnance to this man was too strong for her to brave an altercation with him, well knowing that his retaliation would be pitiless, and his first resource before admitting any charge would be to cast recriminations upon her father.

But one evening Ford had left her alone for a little while, and Drummond had not yet arrived, when Percy sauntered carelessly into the room.

"Good evening, Miss Ford; don't let me disturb you," for she had dropped her work, and he stooped to pick it up—adding as he did so the usual inquiry, " Is your father at home ? "

She laid her hand upon his arm, and said in a hurried eager voice—

" He will be here directly; but Mr. Fenwood, I have long wished to speak to you—listen to me now, and remember my words for God's sake."

He was at a loss to understand her agitation, but seeing she had something to tell, and fearing they might be interrupted, he said nothing, and she resumed rapidly—

" Perhaps I ought not to say this—my father would be angry with me if he knew—but I *cannot* be silent and see wickedness done beneath my eyes. Mr. Fenwood, you believe this man Drummond to be honourable like yourself; but indeed he is not—he is a villain, without conscience, without pity, without remorse."

"My dear Miss Ford, these are strong words—your father does not consider so."

"Do not think of him—do not believe he is bad, though appearances are against him; but what I say is true, as there is a God in Heaven. If you ever touch those dreadful cards again in this house —if you come here at all any more, you will be ruined. They—he, I mean—will never be content till he has drained from you everything you possess. I have warned you—ask me no more."

She rose to leave the room as she spoke, but Percy would have detained her for further explanation had not Drummond and Ford at that moment entered the house together.

"What, Fenwood," said the former, "all alone and as moody as if you were a philosopher? Ford, the reputation of your hospitality is in danger. Why doesn't your fair daughter play the hostess?"

"She has been doing so," said Percy lightly; "but I think she recognised your footstep, Drummond, and, therefore, with great good sense withdrew. Come, are you ready for a game?"

They sat down at the card-table, and Mary's warning was too fresh in Percy's mind for him not to be sharply watchful of his companion's play; but his utmost vigilance could detect nothing irregular, and this went far even on the first evening, to efface the impression of her words.

" Do you think she told him anything ? " said Drummond to his confederate the next time they were alone together; " she hates me as if I were the devil."

" That is a matter of taste," returned the other dryly, " I have no fear for Mary, she will be silent for my sake; unfortunately, she could not strike you without wounding me."

" No, that's true," said Drummond with an ugly smile of satisfaction; "and I don't think there's much danger even if she has told him—he has gone too far to draw back. When he came first he played carelessly, as though the stakes were sixpences and he owned the wealth of the Rothschilds; now his eyes gleam as if it were for life or death. We must put the screw on soon— he's always wanting to play for larger stakes, and I hold him back; but he shall have his own way, it would be cruel to thwart the dear boy's wishes much longer."

The intoxication of desire is at once more subtle and more fatal than alcoholic inebriation; for a little while Percy was haunted by the young girl's words—then their influence became fainter, and finally he forgot them altogether.

CHAPTER III.

" He that dies in an earnest pursuit is like one that is wounded
in hot blood, who, for the time, scarce feels the hurt ; and therefore a mind fixed and bent upon somewhat that is good, doth
avert the dolours of Death ; but above all, believe it, the sweetest
canticle is ' *Nunc dimittis*' when a man hath obtained worthy ends
and expectations. Death hath this also, that it openeth the gate to
good fame, and extinguisheth envy : ' *Extinctus amabitur idem*.'"

LORD BACON.

CONTRARY to general precedent (for in the drama
of life the interest in an actor is rarely felt unless
he is on the stage attracting attention by voice
and gesture) Alice was not forgotten in Seafern.
Perhaps this was partly due to her beauty, of
which the villagers felt justly proud—perhaps to
their ignorance of the great world's philosophy ;
perhaps to the memory of all she had done during
the last two years before her marriage, or perhaps
the fact of her birth which had at first estranged
them from her, now deepened their regret that
her fair face was no longer seen in their midst.
Whatever may have been their motive, her name
was frequently mentioned, and inquiries were

constantly made of Mr. Ellis concerning "Miss Alice and the young squire."

The clergyman found these questions easier to answer' than most of the interrogations his parishioners submitted to him for solution, for Alice corresponded faithfully with him, and was not less anxious for any news of the people amongst whom she had once lived. "I have not been the friend they think me," she had said to him on her wedding day, "but if I were staying here I would really try; and I cannot bear the thought of their forgetting me, or of my losing sight of them altogether; so I look to you to keep the tangible links between us unbroken." He had readily promised, and had duly recorded all the small events of Seafern life, receiving in return messages of sympathy or congratulation.

His letters were very precious to Alice—not that they were strikingly wise or witty, but because they vividly recalled old scenes towards which in her altered life she now felt a wistful longing. They were not wanting either in touches of unstudied pathos and kindly humour; while through them all, as must always be the case with every utterance of a brave true man, there throbbed the noble gentleness of a strong heart.

In her replies she acknowledged the various points of his letters with appreciative interest— with womanly sympathy, and sometimes even with girlish fun. While she was on the Continent she gave many a bright description of what she saw ; but on her return to England the allusions to her own life almost entirely ceased. Of her loneliness in the midst of a crowded city, and her sense of poverty while surrounded by all that wealth can purchase, she of course said nothing. The sharpest sorrows are always veiled ; we waste too much sympathy on tears, while our hearts are cold to the deeper misery which is compelled to play a part and assume a careless gladness in the glare of garish light.

One night about a year after her marriage, Mr. Ellis sat reading one of these letters from Alice, not without a vague sense of misgiving. His perceptions in matters touching womanly feeling were not usually rapid, and there was no distinct phrase in the letter suggesting unhappiness or disappointment; but its general tone lacked buoyancy, he thought, and he could not suppress some uneasy conjectures as to the cause.

"I hope he's kind to her," he murmured, only half-conscious that he was indulging in his old habit of thinking aloud. "There was never any distinct harm in the lad, but he was not worthy of her; and I saw years and years ago that there was danger in that pliable capricious nature of his. I wonder if I had married and had children whether I should have been any wiser than his father was; perhaps not—perhaps not—yet I saw the mistake of this from the beginning."

He read the letter through again very deliberately, and at its conclusion shook his head two or three times before he folded the paper and put it in his pocket.

"No, I'm afraid she's not as happy as she might be," he resumed, "and if it is so, no earthly hand can help her. How one chafes and frets at these troubles when one must watch with folded arms, or make matters worse by attempting to mend them. Another wild night—will the wind never be weary? I can't tell how it is that for the last day or two, the thought of Harry Easton has hardly been out of my mind; what a brave lad he was, and how his pretty young wife loved him; and that cruel sea ended all, and they have slept together in the churchyard for fifteen years. Ah me! it seems like yesterday."

Musing in this disjointed fashion, Mr. Ellis began slowly pacing the room, when a sharp rap at the door disturbed his reverie; and without waiting for permission to come in, his old servant Mary entered—

"I think there must be a wreck, sir, out at sea; I heard the signals just now, and they're getting the lifeboat out."

The sound of a rocket was heard as she spoke; it was not the first, although Mr. Ellis had been too absorbed with his own reflections to hear the former warnings—now, however, he lost no time, but hastily snatching up his hat and overcoat he hurried down to the beach.

It was a rough night, and the waves were running very high; but it was not so stormy as to be anything unusual to one who had seen so many tempests as he. The vessel which had signalled for aid was a small one, and it was not easy at once to perceive what was her danger, as she seemed to be making fair headway, and was not very far from the shore.

"They're gettin' the lifeboat out," said an old sailor to Mr. Ellis, "but I really don't see what's the matter with her. 'Tain't likely that a bit of a boat like that would go fur enough at a time to spring much of a leak; and "—

His words received a terrible interruption—from the deck of the distressed vessel suddenly leaped a red tongue of flame; it disappeared almost instantly, but that one moment left no uncertainty behind.

"Quickly there, my lads," said Mr. Ellis, "are you all ready? You've not a moment to lose."

"We want one more hand, sir," answered their leader; "I believe three of our best men is aboard that very boat."

"I will go," replied the clergyman, springing into the vacant place; "now, my lads, don't waste time—every moment may mean a life."

There was a faint attempt to dissuade him, and two or three younger men offered to go in his place; but he only repeated his last words in so resolute a tone that no one dared to oppose him any longer.

They were all seamen of practised strength and skill, and though there was a strong tide against them, used their oars to such good purpose that in a little while they were near enough to discern more accurately the extent of the danger. The only small boat the barque carried was already cut off from access by the flames, which were rapidly gaining ground. A few men were standing on the deck, alternately making futile attempts to battle with the advancing fire and casting eager glances towards their rescuers, whom the red glare already enabled them to see.

When they came alongside of the burning vessel, an incredibly short space of time was sufficient to transfer the men in such deadly peril to the life-boat.

"Are you all here?" said the man who had taken command of the rescuing party.

One of the sailors they had saved was lying senseless, apparently half suffocated by the smoke; a few more were severely burnt, the rest were comparatively unhurt, and one of these answered the question—

" Yes, we're all here, sir—two, five, six, ten, fourteen. Pull away."

The rowers obeyed, and they had reached about thirty yard's distance from the ship when Mr. Ellis cried in a voice that rang above the noise of wind, sea, and crackling flames—

" You are *not* all here—see there ! "

He pointed as he spoke to the burning deck, on which they could plainly see a woman standing with a baby in her arms.

" It's the skipper's wife," muttered one of the men glancing at the prostrate figure already mentioned, " she was down below, and in the noise and hurry I clean forgot her."

" I thought she was safe aboard," said another, and one of the lifeboat's crew growled in a disgusted tone—

" Thinkin' o' yer own skins in that fashion ! hanged if I think yer worth savin'."

" Silence, lads," said Mr. Ellis in a sharp, stern voice of command ; " make for the ship again, we must save her at any risk."

It was dangerous work, for sparks were flying in all directions, and the flames had seized almost

every inch of the vessel except the spot were the
helpless woman stood; but the strong will was
not to be resisted, and they silently obeyed, since
to have thrown a rope to her they knew was useless,
unless it could be flung right into her hands, and
to do this with any chance whatever of success
while the wind was so high they needed to be
nearer to her.

Half the distance had been reached, but before
this forlorn hope could be tried, the flames caught
the woman's dress, and with a despairing cry she
sprang into the infuriated waves, choosing the
more painless death, since the last thought of
deliverance was gone.

Mr. Ellis's keen eyes had detected the full
extent of the danger before she took the desperate
plunge, and his resolution was formed.   His coat
and boots were already off, and to bind a rope
securely round his waist was the work of a moment.
Without another word, he placed the end in the
hands of the man who sat next him and leaped into
the foaming water.

His companions held their breath in sickening
suspense.   The light of the burning ship was still

bright enough for them to watch that terrible struggle; for of course, the roughness of the sea multiplied the distance twenty times. At last, one wave buried him from their sight so long that they concluded he was lost; when suddenly they perceived him again a dozen yards from them, swimming in their direction with the woman for whose life he had risked his own. Without waiting for any word of command, the men strained every muscle to reach him. A minute that seemed an hour passed, and then he was by the boat's side, and a dozen hands were stretched out to relieve him of his burden.

As his grasp of the woman he had rescued relaxed, and she was lifted into the boat, another immense wave broke upon them—in that fatal moment he was borne away.

They had still the rope he had bound round him, and they hauled in hastily; but their worst fears were realised—they recovered only his lifeless body. The force of the waves in one terrible instant had literally beaten him to death.

"He's dead!" said one of the sailors with a sob, he made no attempt to conceal—"him as was worth the lot o' us; row in lads, we must save ourselves; but I'm blest if I care who's drownded now."

The woman he had saved soon recovered from the stunning blows of the waves, though her brain still seemed delirious from the horrors through which she had passed. Seeing that the child she had clasped to her bosom with the strength of despair, when menaced by sea and fire, was safe, she loosened her hold and put it in a sailor's arms; then bending over her deliverer, she cried hoarsely—

"He isn't dead—I could feel his heart beat if my hands were not so cold," and she strove by word, by caress, and even by a wild faint song, to restore him to consciousness.

"She's crazed," said the man to whom she had given her baby; but he held it tenderly, and no attempt was made to disturb her.

On the shore an eager crowd was waiting their return, and when they were near enough to hear they were greeted with loud and enthusiastic cheers; but no man among the crew had heart or voice to answer, and when the story of that evening's rescue was told, no one, despite their success, wondered at their silence.

The sufferers received prompt attention, and the lifeless form was carried to the home which the villagers had for years looked upon as the one place of all the world where help and sympathy were certain.

That night in Seafern everyone mourned the loss of a friend—for there was not a cottage he had left unvisited, not a heart he had left uncheered. His death caused slight remark beyond the narrow limits of his own parish—he had never distinguished himself as a theologian or a preacher, and his name was quite unknown in the great ecclesiastical circles; therefore his memory was not perpetuated by elegy or marble—nor did he receive that apotheosis of mediocrity, a biography written by a religious hero-worshipper. But a simple grave in the Seafern churchyard tells that George Ellis was priest of that parish for thirty years, and until the last child who knew him sleeps in the same quiet resting-place, there will be hearts that gratefully recall the noble faith and large-hearted devotion with which he lived and died.

CHAPTER IV.

Lady, 'tis yours to save him—I have failed,
For I am nothing to him; and my words
Were powerless as echoes of the past,
To souls that worship gold; but you are fair,
And God has writ a poem in your eyes,
Which all who read must love—he most of all:
Speak then with sweet persuasive eloquence,
And he will listen till the fatal spell
Which binds him now is broken.

THE first intimation Alice received of the events recorded in the preceding chapter was conveyed in a letter from one of the lifeboat's crew, who was old enough to remember the affection which had existed between Mr. Ellis and her father. Most of the Seafern villagers were more at home in handling a rope or an oar than in guiding a pen; and the account was given in a rambling manner, with strange turns of phrase, peculiarities of grammar, and persistently phonetic orthography; but to Alice, who knew the people, this only gave realistic force to a tragic tale of devotion and death. In the county newspaper which she saw the next day, there was a full account of the scene with much laboured pathos, studied eulogy, and irrelevant quotation; but although she read with eagerness every word relating to her dead friend's last deed of heroism, the simple language of the sailor seemed the more fitting record.

She said little, even to Percy, of what this new sorrow meant to her; but her heart ached wearily with the knowledge that she had lost her last friend—that henceforth she had no part in the little fishing village where she had been born, which she could be certain was her own. She had treasured his letters too, not only because it was pleasant to read them, and sweet to conjure up by their aid old scenes and familiar faces; but because they had a strange influence and encouragement for her. Didactic correspondence she would probably [have resented, for there were still some strong touches of proud self-will in her disposition; but their teaching was of a far more subtle character, and braced her for duty, as the cool breath of mountain air refreshes the student, weary of poring over books and endless calculations.

She had been grateful for any help, but now

that her need was greatest it was taken away
from her. When a mistake has been made, life is
never satisfied with pointing the fact out once,
but confronts us with the dreary consequences of
the error at every step we take; and each day
Alice saw more clearly that from her husband she
could no longer expect even the love of a dear
friend.

It is sad to watch the growth of physical disease
—to see the pale cheek daily growing thinner, the
form becoming more emaciated; and the sufferer's
hold on the world and its interests hopelessly re-
laxing—for the dawn to reveal the terrible truth,
that the hours of darkness have come like thieves,
and borne away something more of power, of
energy, or of grace; but the progress of moral
disease is sadder still; and it was becoming
evident, not only to Alice, but to more careless ob-
servers, that the latent evil in Percy's character
was increasing; and its impulsive goodness
diminishing every day.

The effect was palpable, but she was still
ignorant of the cause. Had she known the truth
earlier, she might perhaps have saved him, for she

was stronger than he, not only in heart but in mind and will; as it was, however, she offered little opposition to his actions, and although his constant absence from home at night grieved and perplexed her, she never asked the reason. In this she may have laid herself open to the charge of dulness in perception; but simultaneously with the discovery that she could only give him a divided love (which in the noblest sense is not love at all), she had formed the resolution to atone for this as far as was in her power by unquestioning submission. This was her leading motive for silence, and (for in the soul's alchemy fire and snow often mingle strangely together) she may have been too proud to solicit a confidence he would not give her unasked.

One evening some months later, she was sitting alone thinking of these things, and wondering for the thousandth time if she was at all to blame, and if any further sacrifice of inclination could give her back any of the exultant gladness she had once known, when a servant entered the room and observed laconically—

"Young woman waiting downstairs, mum."

" What does she want? "

" She says she wants to see you, mum, on a most partickler subject."

" Show her up," said Alice indifferently, not doubting that the individual thus mysteriously announced was charged with no more important business than a message from her dressmaker.

The man obeyed, and ushered in with little ceremony a girl about Alice's own age, very plainly and neatly dressed, with a face that although not actually pretty, was pleasant to look at ; and by its gentle goodness would generally command confidence and respect. She seemed rather abashed by the costliness which characterised the room, and by finding in Alice, a lady so beautiful and finely dressed, and would have remained standing. Yielding however to persuasion, and evidently reassured by the sweetness of Alice's voice, she sat down and said simply—

" It seems a great liberty that I have taken in coming here, and now that I have done it, I almost wonder at my own courage ; but I hope you can help me, and I have come to implore your aid."

"If I can do anything I will gladly," answered Alice kindly; "but my power is not great."

Her visitor looked incredulously at her, with a glance that said plainly—"Is it possible beauty and wealth can be impotent?" but she only replied—"You are good and kind—I was certain of that directly I heard your voice; but it is not for my-self I wish to plead—it is for you, and for your husband."

"My husband!" Alice echoed the words with a sudden feeling of dread. Had she guarded her secret to so little purpose, that strangers held the clue to it?

"It is difficult for you to believe me, and it has cost me a long hard effort to speak; but I dare not be silent any longer. Wrong and wickedness are being done before my eyes—they are making me old and miserable—they keep me awake at night, or haunt my dreams like ghosts. God knows I am innocent of it all—I have tried to stop it, but I can do nothing —I have warned your husband, but he has not heeded me—my last appeal is to you."

"I do not understand you."

"I am talking wildly," said the girl, "but I fancied you must have some suspicion of this. Tell me one thing—is not Mr. Fenwood generally away from home till late at night ? "

" Yes."

" Do you know where he goes ? "

Alice buried her face in her hands, with a bitter sense of humiliation, and did not answer.

" I will tell you then—my name is Mary Ford, and this is my address—you may need it some day, so I have written it on this piece of paper. Mr. Fenwood comes to my father's house almost every night now; and—and always for one thing—gambling."

The last word struck Alice like a poisoned arrow; she sprang to her feet with a cry of pain, and her face was so white that Mary Ford was frightened at the effect of her own words.

" Gambling—he," she exclaimed, " you must be mistaken—he is too good for that—it cannot be true."

" I would to God it were false," said Mary, in a tone of misery which no acting could have counterfeited.

There was silence between them for a few moments, during which interval there crowded on the minds of each, thoughts of pain too deep for utterance. At length Alice said almost fiercely—

" Do you measure the meaning of your words ? If this is true Percy is cruelly wronged, and the guilt is not his, but your father's."

" It seems so," pleaded Mary. " I know appearances are terribly against him; otherwise I should have spoken long ago; but he has worse companions than my father. There is one man who professes to be his friend, who will stop at nothing —who will never be content till he has ruined him, and robbed him of everything he holds dear in life. Above all things, warn him against that man—his name is Henry Drummond."

With these words Mary rose as if to go, but Alice detained her—

" Stay," she said, " you have told me of danger but not how I can prevent it."

" He must love you," returned Mary simply, " and there is a strength about you, as if you were accustomed to be obeyed. Use your utmost influence—warn—plead—and reason with him. Entreat him by all he holds most sacred, never to enter our house again. Say there is a curse upon it, and upon us—tell him he is staking not money only, but hope, happiness, and your own heart."

Alice observed her narrowly.

"How can you live in such a house as you describe?" she asked.

"Because he is my father—because there is much—indeed—indeed there is very much, that is good in him—he is always kind to me, and he does not know how much harm there is in a life he has been led to adopt by slow degrees, and many causes. Even to his sin there are always limits—he plays honourably—I know that, for he has told me so often, and he would not lie; but the other man is pitiless, and hopelessly bad. I have warned you—may you be more successful than I have been."

She inclined her head in mute farewell, when Alice again stopped her and said, taking both her hands in hers—

"I will try—but I have little hope; if I had known this months ago, I think I could have succeeded—now I fear it is too late. Whatever your surroundings may be, I trust you, and believe that you are good—you are the only creature on earth who has held out a hand to save him. May God bless you for it—will you wear this ring as a pledge of my gratitude?"

It was a costly trinket, and Mary hesitated; but Alice pressed it on her finger, saying—

"It is a memento—nothing else. No one but you knows that I am wretched, but you have torn the veil away—it is idle to attempt concealment to-night. I have few friends—none to whom I can look for help—remember this when you look at the ring—and pray for me—perhaps God will hear your prayers sooner than mine."

She suffered Mary to leave her, and then sitting down once more, tried to collect her scattered thoughts, and face the future calmly. She could not doubt that evening's revelation, which at once explained many things that before had baffled her —she understood now the change in Percy's character—she saw clearly how his gaiety had been clouded, and his spirits alternately un-naturally high, and moodily depressed—she no

longer wondered that a temper once easy, almost
to sweetness, should have grown irritable without
any apparent cause; yet her heart had never felt
so tender to him as now. "Poor boy," she
thought, "if I had loved him as I ought to have
done, I should have intuitively divined this, and
warned him long ago. I should not mind the loss
of money much—what happiness has all this extravagance brought me? I am a fisherman's
daughter, and could surrender riches without a
sigh; but where will his infatuation end?—it will
break his heart, and mine too."

CHAPTER V.

"There are skies so dull and leaden, that we long for storm winds
       stirring—
There is peace so cold and bitter, that we almost welcome strife."
                                        ADELAIDE PROCTOR.

IT was past twelve when Percy returned that
night, and Alice in accordance with her invariable custom when he was late, had sent the servants to bed. As he glanced at the house, whose
darkness was relieved only by a single unextin-
guished light, he at once inferred she was waiting up for him, and although he was in an
unusually good humour (for fortune that evening
had been in his favour) he could not wholly repress an uneasy feeling of self-reproach.

"Poor Alice," he thought, "it is too bad of
me to leave her so much alone. I wonder if she
cares—she used to complain if anything annoyed
her ; but now she is always silent about herself.
Well—well, a man must sow his wild oats—by-

and-by I shall be tired of cards and billiards, and then I'll become a model husband."

He unlocked the street door with his latch-key, and went straight to the room where he knew she would be. She had not heard his light step, and in the first glimpse he caught of her on opening the door, he saw she was sitting alone, with her face buried in her hands, her long hair falling in careless beauty, and her whole attitude indicating the deepest grief. As he entered she looked up and tried to smile; but he saw at once that she was very pale, and unusually agitated.

"Why Allie," he said gently, advancing towards her, and laying his hand lightly on her shoulder, "you look tired and ill dear. You should have been in bed an hour ago."

She did not immediately answer in words, but threw her arms round him, and laid her cheek against his, an unwonted action for her, who rarely gave an unsolicited caress.

"Dear Percy," she said simply, "I do not mean to reproach you, but could you not have trusted me?"

"Trusted you Alice—what do you mean?"

"I know all," she answered. "I have heard to-night what it is that calls you so constantly from home—and I think my heart will break."

He started from her embrace, and irresolutely paced two or three times up and down the room; then he returned to her and said, still trying to speak indifferently—

"You are talking enigmas Allie—you have been dreaming, and are only half awake now."

"I *have* been dreaming," she replied, "of ruin, of misery, of dishonour. Do not put me off with evasive answers—I am your wife—you loved me once, and—"

"Once Alice!" he echoed, "I love you now, a thousand times better than any woman—ay, or any man either, in the world."

"If it is so," she continued, "you will not resist my entreaties, when I plead with you as if for life. A girl named Mary Ford has been here to-night—she has told me everything: she sees the peril that you are in, although from her duty to her father she has striven to close her eyes. Percy, I know nothing of the world, I am only a village girl who has lived the greater part of her life among simple fishermen, and is herself not much wiser; but I am not blind, and I cannot hide from myself what the end of all this must be. Your character is being ruined—I hardly know my old playfellow he is so changed—you are not happy: this terrible excitement is eating your heart away. Command me to do anything not wrong, from which my inclinations most shrink, and I will obey you like a slave; but if as you say, you still love me—if you still care to look at the poor beauty you used to praise so highly, tear yourself away from these men, who have such cruel designs upon you; and happiness may not be a lost word with us after all."

He was touched by her appeal; but it would have needed a stronger hand than his to snap in a moment, chains which had been slowly forged through so many months. He sat down beside her, and taking her hand in his, said in a reassuring tone—

" Dear Alice, you have been needlessly alarming yourself. Mary Ford is a very good girl, I dare say; but she has mistaken her vocation in life. She should have been a dramatic authoress;

then her ingenious tragedies wrought out of nothing, might have been interesting; as it is, they are apt to be inconvenient. I'll be bound she said all sorts of dreadful things about Drummond."

"Yes; she warned us earnestly against that man."

"I knew it," returned Percy triumphantly. "I believe he made love to her once, and not being to her taste, it was the easiest thing in the world for her to persuade herself into the conviction that he was an incarnate fiend. Now as a matter of fact, he's nothing of the kind; he's well connected, has been an officer in the army, and is really very clever and amusing. I don't mean to say he's a hero, or quite the sort of a man one would select for a missionary, or advise to become the super-intendent of a Sunday-school; but then, neither am I for that matter; yet I don't think it would be quite just to call me a villain."

Alice had anticipated a reply of this nature, and was not deceived by it; but she resolved to say nothing until he should have concluded, and he resumed in a more confident tone—

"Well then, as to the gambling—it's an ugly word; but what does it amount to in reality? Simply this, that life being on the whole rather a tame and stupid affair, one must vary it with a certain amount of excitement. Everyone admits this in practice or theory, and the form which it takes is a mere question of taste and disposition. Now my fair mother confessor, I never professed to be stronger than other people; but I don't think you can blame a fellow unless he goes out of his way to be worse than his neighbours. I've not talked to you about these things, because I thought, they mightn't quite suit your views; but I won't deny your charges altogether. On the contrary, I'll admit frankly that I've betted occasionally, and staked a little money now and then on cards and billiards: before I leave the confessional, say which is it to be, absolution or excommunication."

"Oh! Percy how can you speak so lightly of such things?"

"Because they are not worth serious thought. The idea of my being ruined by them is simply absurd: you know I always hated calculations; so

I cannot tell you exactly what this fancy you think so terrible, has cost me; but it can't be much. Ruin from such small play as mine, is like what people say about coffee and tobacco being poison; perhaps if men lived to the age of the patriarchs there might be something in it— as it is, after drinking oceans of coffee, and smoking thousands of cigars, a man won't complain if he feels a little failing energy on his ninetieth birthday."

Alice felt her heart grow heavy with the sense of hopelessness. This careless good-humour which would not see a truth, was harder to encounter than any display of anger would have been. She said sadly—

"When I was a child I used to wish I were a man, that I might be a sailor. I have learnt much since then, but I chafe at the sense of a woman's impotence still. Dear Percy—dearer to me since the knowledge of your danger and mine, than you were when we were first married, and your whole life seemed devoted to satisfying my caprices—you do not believe your own words, and they cannot deceive me. Do you think the alteration in you has escaped my notice? Do you imagine I can see all that was attractive in your character passing away, and feel no anxiety as to the cause?"

"I'm growing older perhaps."

"Time does not age men in a few months: you say life is tame and stupid," (her lip quivered as she repeated his words, but her voice did not falter) "perhaps that is my fault. Tell me any thing you would wish different in me; and I will strive with every faculty of heart and brain to change it."

"That is a large promise, but I don't happen to want anything altered, except that pale sad look of yours which doesn't suit you half so well as a smile. Come now, be equally frank with me— what can I do to put all these morbid anticipations out of your head?"

"Promise me you will never see these men again."

"You are unreasonable Alice," he answered gaily, "one can't cut acquaintances in that summary fashion; still I'll think of it, and give you an answer in the morning. I'm not such a selfish

brute as you consider me, and if it had been anything else you had wanted, I'd have given it you
with pleasure. This is more difficult; but I'll see
about it and let you know."

Next morning he said to her—

"I can't promise to do exactly what you asked,
but there was much truth in your words dear—
after all you are right. I have not been happier
since those confounded cards mixed themselves up
so much with my affairs; it would be well if 'I
gave them up, and upon my honour I will try."

Alice was obliged to be contented with this,
and strove to believe an intention she knew to be
genuine might usher in brighter days; but Drummond's prophecy had come true, and the passion
for gambling had obtained tyrannic dominion over
his dupe. The power of the human will is almost
infinite in its possibilities; and there have been
men who have conquered even more fatal despot-
ism than this, by mere force of iron resolution;
but they have been made of sterner stuff than
Percy Fenwood, and have been inspired by heroic
determination, not by fitful impulse.

He had promised to try, and he kept his word;

for about a week Drummond and Ford saw nothing of him, and for some time after that his visits were less frequent, and he evinced a decided disinclination for high stakes. But the gamblers never doubted the issue, and they were right—the utmost the weak swimmer can do is to keep himself from sinking, and to suffer the direction of his progress to be determined by the course of the stream.

Alice had said that the end of this would be to break her heart; but she was young and strong, and although her weary life grew daily darker—though sunset only ushered in a night when her lonely thoughts were crowded with terrible fancies, and dread imaginations she dared not have shaped in words—though the dawn never brought her a ray of hope, that divine gift which so often remains when time has robbed the soul of all other wealth; physical life throbbed with ardent vigour still, and she did not die.

"What a happy girl you must be," her Cousin Ethel said to her one day, "you never have headache or neuralgia, or anything of that kind—you live in a fine house—you have as much money as you like, everyone admires you, and your husband worships you. He is so handsome too, and has the most irresistible way of paying a compliment : positively if I told you half the things he says to me when I meet him (which by the way isn't as often as it used to be), you would be jealous."

Alice smiled rather bitterly and changed the subject. She knew she was a poor actress, and if she attempted to sustain a false part she must sooner or later betray the truth; but there was safety in silence, and behind this broad shield she hid from all who knew her the secret of her wrongs.

The winter and the spring passed away—in the summer she had hoped to go to Seafern, to revisit the old scenes and prove to all the people that she had not forgotten them ; but now Mr. Ellis was dead, and so dark a shadow had fallen upon her own life, she had not the courage to return to her old home, lest the associations and memories it must awaken should prove too painful, and the simple-hearted villagers who had known her as a happy thoughtless child should read her secret in her eyes.

Therefore she went with Percy to Scarborough,

and found in the gay scene of fashion but small
variation from the dreariness of home. True, the
air was keen and bracing, and the majestic sea
was there; but in such company it seemed to her
(accustomed to associate it only with tragic
grandeur) strangely out of place, and the necessity
for dissimulation was greater even than it had
been in London, where of late they had seen little
company.

Shortly after their return they were sitting
together at the breakfast-table one morning, each
following separate occupations, quite in accordance
with matrimonial usage. Percy was glancing
carelessly over his letters, and Alice was trying to
read a newspaper published in the town nearest to
Seafern, which found its way into the house
despite its modest pretensions to literary merit,
for the sake of local news. The leading article
was an enthusiastic eulogy on the abilities of a
vestryman, who having made a large fortune by
the sale of candles, was condescendingly devoting
some of his superfluous leisure to the consideration
of narrowing workhouse expenses. The panegyric
on this worthy was not particularly lively, and

Alice was laying the paper listlessly down when an advertisement in another column arrested her attention, and she exclaimed—

"Percy, can this be true? Is it possible that Seafern Hall is to be sold?"

"Oh, yes; didn't I tell you? The place was going to rack and ruin; it cost money to keep it up, and we should never have gone there. A speculator made me an offer for it, and I should have been a fool to lose the chance."

"I thought it was entailed."

"So did I until it became my property; but it never has been. How such a dismal old place could have remained so long in the family is more than I can understand; however, it's going to the hammer now, and a good job too."

Alice never interfered in his business arrangements, and this was no affair of hers, so she merely said, rather sadly—

"And the furniture and paintings—what of them?"

"Well, you know we brought the paintings you liked best here; if there's any other you particularly want, I'll have it bought for you. As for the furniture, it's mere old-fashioned lumber, and I shall be glad to get rid of it. Good-bye, Alice, I have an appointment this morning with my solicitor."

So the last frail link which bound her to Seafern was broken; save for the sacred memories buried in the secret chambers of her heart. She wondered whether this sale of a home which had been in his family for generations meant merely carelessness, or the fact that the losses he had spoken of as trifling made retrenchment of some kind imperative. She could not tell, but her life seemed heavy, like the air before a thunder-storm; and she knew not when the dreaded crash would come.

CHAPTER VI.

First Citizen—   Our fair conspiracy
Which was to yield such profit, is disclosed.
*Second Citizen—*Then no resource remains for us but flight.

IT was a dark evening in November, when the air did not belie the season by any impertinent attempts at cheerfulness. On the contrary, the heavy fog which rested on the muddy streets was so persistently depressing, and the muffled-up pedestrians had so dejected an expression, that any spectator (even though he had just been roused from an enchanted slumber of a century or so, and consequently become slightly confused as to his exact position with regard to time and country) would at once have realised that the city was London, and the time the month inseparably associated in the English mind with bronchitis, Lord Mayor's day, and the smouldering effigy of Guy Fawkes.

William Ford's house, standing in one of the darkest streets, did not look particularly inviting, although its display of gas made it flaringly prominent. But the question of appearance had never been an important consideration in the gambler's mind; and that evening as he sat alone with Henry Drummond, he seemed to be occupied with very serious reflections. The two men smoked silently for some time, then Drummond said—

"The game goes well, eh?"

Ford nodded, but did not speak; and his companion pursued—

"He promised to bring the money to-night, and a man who brings three thousand pounds with him is always welcome. Do you know, Ford, I think it was devilish good-natured of me to agree to our going halves in the profits—I found the fish, I baited the hook, I took all the trouble of angling, and now that the prize is nearly landed I think it ought to be mine."

"I think otherwise," said Ford quietly.

"Of course you do—confounded old Jew without a conscience as you are. Well, I've promised, and I'll keep my word—honour and liberality have always been my weak points; but hush! here he comes."

As he spoke, Percy entered the room, and greeted them with something of his old careless good humour.

"What a night it is," he said, as he removed his greatcoat, "I wouldn't have come here if I hadn't promised to pay you that money; but it's been accumulating some time, so I didn't like to keep you waiting any longer. See here," he added, producing a large pocket-book filled with bank-notes, "we'll reckon up at the end of this evening's play. I have brought double the amount I owe you, and I mean to court fortune to-night by boldness. Is Morton coming?"

This was a friend of Percy's who occasionally made a fourth at the card-table, but being of a more prudent disposition he was less frequent in his visits; and Drummond answered the question in the negative.

"Well, I'm not sorry," resumed Percy, "he's always afraid of high stakes, and I mean to test to-night whether there is any truth in the saying that fortune favours the brave. There—I'm warmer now, and ready for anything you like."

His companions had looked hungrily at the

notes when he displayed them, and exchanged significant glances. Drummond laughed, and feigned unwillingness for the test.

"If I were not bound in honour to give you your revenge, I think I should refuse to play to-night. The luck has been running against you rather lately, but nothing on earth can stand against desperate pluck. No matter for that— since you are ready, so am I," and he took his seat at the card-table.

They played for some time with varying success —the final result being that Percy was slightly the loser.

"I'm tired of this child's play," he said impatiently, "come, Drummond, let's have a stake worth winning. I've made the debt exactly three thousand pounds—I'll play you double or quits."

"No," said Ford, interposing with genuine concern, "this business is growing too grave. I can't have such desperate playing in my house."

"Nonsense," said Drummond, "I accept Mr. Fenwood's challenge; if you don't want to take a hand you needn't—we will determine the issue alone, by cribbage or billiards."

The elder man offered no further opposition, but finding his protest was disregarded determined to have a share in the spoil. The first game of the rubber Percy won—the second he lost; and the third seemed going in his favour when Drummond, taking advantage of a moment when his opponent's eyes were fixed on his own hand, dropped one of the cards he held beneath the table and hastily snatched another from the pack.

The exchange was performed with such dexterity, that his partner did not observe it; but Percy looking up at that moment detected him in the act, and flinging down his cards sprang to his feet with an oath.

"You are a liar and a thief," he cried white with rage, "and I have been fool enough to trust you. It was an evil day for me that ever I saw your face, and I will thrash you as you deserve."

He sprang upon the gambler as he spoke, and seized him by the throat; his attack was so unexpected, that for a moment he had the advantage in the struggle; but he was no match either in strength or skill for Drummond, as a single minute was long enough to prove. Stung by the bitter words, enraged at the knowledge that his dupe had at last broken the snares, and goaded to fury by the sense of detected fraud, he freed himself from Percy's grasp, and struck him with all the force he could muster.

Percy reeled, staggered and fell heavily, striking his head against the iron fender; giving only one groan, and then lying motionless and unconscious on the floor.

All this was done so quickly, that William Ford's slow movements had been unequal to the slightest interference; he had risen from the table however, and now said, his face white with apprehension,

" You've killed him."

" Humbug," retorted the other, bending over the prostrate form, " he'll be as well as you or I in half an hour. He's a little stunned; but it will do him no harm to lose some of his hot blood; and the blow may teach him to be more civil in future."

" What the devil did you cheat for? " said Ford anxiously, " it was cutting your own throat, for the game is up now; besides being against my rules."

"Confound you and your rules—see here;" as he spoke he picked up the pocket-book which had fallen in the wrestle. "There's no time for moralising," he said rapidly "here are six thousand pounds—the game is up as you say, but I am not going to lose these. It will be some minutes at all events before our dear friend recovers, and when he does, he will hardly be in condition to give chase. I'm off to America—will you come with me?"

His companion hesitated—

"Do you mean to leave him here?" he faltered.

"Would you have us wait till he's well enough to get us into trouble? I tell you there's no time for foolery. Are you coming or not?"

"My daughter—" said Ford still wavering.

Drummond muttered an oath between his clenched teeth—

"Good-bye," he said, "I'm off, if you have to end your days in the shady retirement of a prison, don't blame me."

There was a terrible battle at that moment being fought in William Ford's heart. Love for his daughter was strong, and compassion for the helplessness of the man he had assisted to ruin was not without a certain power; but avarice was mightier than both, and the fear of consequences could not be silenced.

"I will go with you," he said, "stay only one moment."

He seized a pen and paper, and wrote a few lines with a trembling hand; these he addressed to his daughter, and leaving the note on the table, informed his impatient companion that he was ready. Drummond without another word, turned out the gas, and they hurried into the street together.

CHAPTER VII.

At last the black-lipped tempest speaks in words
Of deep toned thunder; while the heavy sky
Grows red with sudden flashes of swift light—
Majestic, grand, and fatal; yet the air
Will be the sweeter for it, and the flow'rs
Will gain thereby a fairer blush and smile—
The grass will wave more gaily, and the lark
May sing a richer welcome to the dawn,
Than earth e'er heard before.

On the same evening, Mary Ford little dreaming
what was happening so near her, was sitting upstairs reading in her own room, which although
small and very plainly furnished, seemed to have
gained something of her individuality, and was
consequently the pleasantest part of the house.
Here she spent most of her leisure time, and she
had contrived by a few skilful touches to make the
apartment which was her bedroom, boudoir, studio,
and library, pleasing and graceful. There were
one or two sketches of her own upon the walls—
not possessing any remarkable artistic merit, but
recalling sunny meadows and shady woods, or the

sweet serenity of gentle faces. Her bookshelves
too, contained no scholarly indications, but they
had some works that were beyond all price to
Mary, though she had only had to save a few
shillings in order to become rich by their possession.

In the day time she worked hard, for she was a
dressmaker's assistant, preferring any drudgery to
absolute dependence on her father's way of life;
and at night her leisure could scarcely be called
freedom, for it was haunted always by apprehen-
sions of impending ruin or disgrace. But although
an innocent heart will suffer by reason of its
goodness, it will find stray gleams of sunshine on
the cloudiest days; and sometimes when her heart
was heavy Mary would enter this quiet sanctuary,
and yielding herself up to the influence of some
great master in the domain of fancy, would forget
her own sorrows for a little while and be happy.
She was a poor critic in all except her recognition
of the true and the false—there her instincts never
failed.

That evening she was reading "Evangeline,"
and the simple story had taken such strong pos-

session of her mind, and the Acadian maiden's wanderings had seemed so real to her, that when at last she found the dying lover, to whom her heart had been through life unwaveringly conse- crated, Mary could hardly read the closing words of the poem through her tears; and although she believed herself to be quite unimaginative, except by sympathy with the thoughts of others, her fancy wandered far away with that tender regret which has no bitterness in it.

Her reflections were disturbed by a church clock striking the hour of midnight; and she was im- mediately recalled to practical life. Twelve o'clock was the limit her father had fixed for keeping the house open; and she had never known him to ex- ceed it. It was her custom to go down to him when he was alone—to talk to him if he was in the humour for conversation, and finally to see that all the windows were fastened; and the doors locked, and to put out the lights before herself re- tiring to rest. Therefore she waited a little while, listening for the sound of the street door being shut; but all was quiet, and she concluded that her father's visitors, whoever they were, must have

already left him while she was absorbed in the
story of the farmer's daughter of Grand-Pré.

With this idea she left her room, and looking
over the bannisters, saw to her surprise that the
lights below were already extinguished. Unable
to imagine the cause of this, she lit a candle and
having satisfied herself that her father was not upstairs, went straight to the room where she was
most likely to find him. It seemed to be empty,
but she noticed that the window was still open,
and advancing to shut it, she observed a dark stain
on the floor. Stooping down to examine it more
closely, she gave a low cry of horror at the discovery that it was blood.

A moment later and she perceived Percy lying
lifeless as it seemed to her, beside the fire. With
a fear at her heart that was shapeless and terrible,
she knelt down beside him, and found with un-
speakable thankfulness that her worst fears were
untrue.

"Thank God he breathes!" she murmured,
"but where is my father, and why have they left
him alone?"

As she rose to her feet, and tried to consider

what was best to be done, she caught sight of the letter on the table addressed to herself; she opened it eagerly, and read as follows, in what was evidently her father's handwriting, though the scarcely legible characters, gave evidence of having been penned at a moment of great excitement and agitation.

"Do not believe I have had any part in the attack on young Fenwood; of that I am wholly innocent, whatever other guilt may lie at my door. He fell in a struggle with Drummond, which he himself provoked; but there are many reasons why it is not well for me to remain in England. I am going abroad to-night, for a while at all events, and will write you word of my further movements. Until you hear from me again you had better still live in the old house; you will find money enough for your present wants in my cash-box—you know where the key is kept. Burn this.—W. F."

"Abroad," she thought, "and without a word of farewell—why should he leave me like this? What has he done that he must quit the country like a felon? And Mr. Fenwood, too, how can I save him without betraying my father? Oh, God! I have no hope but in Thee; help me now at this time of direst need."

She wheeled the sofa close to Percy's unconscious figure, and tried to lift him upon it; but her strength was unequal to the task. Her efforts were not fruitless, however, for they seemed to rouse him from his stupor; he opened his eyes and looked at her with a fixed gaze of bewildered wonder.

"Where am I?" he asked faintly. "I feel weak and ill—how did I come here?"

Mary answered his questions as best she could, and a confused remembrance of what had passed that evening seemed to dawn upon him. He tried to rise, but was still too weak, and would have fallen if her arms had not saved him. With her assistance he managed to get on the sofa, and during a few minutes' silence, which she was afraid to disturb, seemed trying to collect his scattered thoughts. At length he said in a tone more like his usual voice—

"Where is your father?"

"Gone."

"And Drummond?"

"I do not know."

There was another silence, during which Mary regarded him anxiously, unable to decide what she ought to do. She was afraid to leave him alone, even to bring a surgeon; and dreaded revealing the secret of his presence there lest it should criminate her father. On the other hand, she dared not remain inactive, and was more than half resolved to risk everything in the attempt to save him. At that moment, however, she heard wheels, and hastily going to the window saw that the sound came from a stray cab returning home after some late fare. Signing to the man to wait a moment, she returned to Percy, and said with quick determination—

"I was afraid there would be no means of conveyance in the streets so late as this; but there is a cab outside the house now. Are you well enough to return home? I will go with you."

"Yes," he said, "that will be best; but there is no need to bring you out, Miss Ford. I shall be quite well directly I get into the fresh air."

Mary did not stay to answer this, but putting on her hat and cloak offered him her arm, which he took silently, and leaning heavily upon her reached the cab without much difficulty.

"Gen'l'man's took ill, I s'pose, Miss," said the man, observing his feeble steps.

"Yes," said Mary hurriedly, giving him the address; "do not drive too fast."

The cabman gave a grin of acquiescence. "It'll be minded in the fare, I hope, Miss," he observed plaintively, and receiving a hasty assent he drove away, probably meditating with the pensive philosophy of his class, what the meaning of this expedition might be.

Percy bore the journey better than Mary had dared to hope; the cool air, for it had ceased raining and the fog had cleared away, seemed to revive him, and his companion began to think her alarm groundless and his hurt only trifling after all. Towards the end of the drive, however, he showed signs of exhaustion, and Mary proposed that she should run on and prepare his wife for his arrival.

Percy was at first unwilling that she should do

this; but she was firm, and he was not strong enough for argument, so at length he yielded, and she hastened on to fulfil her intention.

The door was opened by Alice herself, who had as usual, sent the servants to bed, and who immediately read in Mary's face that she was the bearer of ill news.

"Tell me the worst," she said quickly, " I am strong enough to bear it."

" Dear Mrs. Fenwood," replied Mary, taking her hand with girlish sympathy, " do not be alarmed— there is no 'worst' to tell. Your husband has met with a slight accident—very slight, I trust; he will be here directly. I came in the cab with him—it is quite near; but I thought it best to come and tell you first that you might be calm when he arrived."

" What kind of accident ? "

" He fell and struck his head, and "—

"Who did it?" said Alice quickly, observing her hesitation.

" Henry Drummond—the man I warned you against."

" The friend he trusted," thought Alice bitterly;

but she said nothing, for at that moment the cab turned the corner, and before it reached the house she was standing on the pavement, eager with her own eyes to learn the worst.

"There's nothing the matter, Allie," said Percy in a tone which belied his words. "I shall have a headache for a day or two, perhaps; but you needn't be frightened." He took her arm as he spoke and entered the house, but almost fainted on the threshold. Alice carried him into the dining-room in her strong loving arms, and laid him gently on the couch. Their old relations seemed to have returned—he was no longer the husband who had wronged her by neglect, and wearied her by his reckless ind ifference: but the childish playfellow she had loved so well. Mary stood watching her with adm iration—

"Is there nothing more I can do?" she asked.

Alice gave her the address o f the nearest doctor, to whose house the cabman to ok her with more alacrity than was his wont, for Alice had forgotten nothing, and he had received a liberal fare.

"Blest if I know what to make of this yer concern," he soliloquised, "wot's that young cove been a doin' with his 'ed, and who be these young women? be they his sisters, or be one of 'em his wife? Or is he a Morming, and married to both on 'em? That young woman in the 'ouse seemed no end of a swell, but she lifted that chap like a reg'lar good 'un. Well, it's a rum start all the way, but the world's made up of queer games; " and with this profound reflection, which in a slightly different form, is the conclusion enunciated by more abstruse philosophers, he took Mary first to the surgeon's and then to her own house, and touching his hat at the door with a comical mixture of respect, familiarity, and confused conjecture, left her.

The doctor soon arrived, and after examining Percy, and hearing as much of that night's adventure as it was necessary to reveal, looked grave, and said he should like further advice to be taken. Of the patient's prospects of speedy recovery, he would not speak explicitly; he hoped for the best, but could predict more confidently the result of this on the morrow.

" The storm has come at last," said Alice to herself, when the surgeon had left her and Percy had sunk into a quiet sleep. "Perhaps it is the prelude to brighter days—perhaps after he recovers we may be to each other what we once were, and all these dreary months may seem only like a morbid dream; poor boy, this rough awakening may save him from a worse shipwreck. He will care more for me after I have been enabled by this opportunity to prove that he is still dear to me—that I do not forget old days; that I am loyal to my promise to his dead father and my marriage vows."

CHAPTER VIII.

I waken from a troubled sleep,
　　For such I hold the recent years,
　　When oft I gave you cause for tears,
And made your heart too sad to weep.

For now I deem the tale of wrong
　　A vision of the restless night,
　　Whose murmur at the touch of light
Grows to the gladness of a song.

And you and I are children, sweet,
　' Untouched by thought of future care;
　　For wave and sky are blue and fair,
And earth a playground for our feet.

We gather pebbles on the beach—
　　We make a playmate of the sea—
　　We find in every bird and tree
A golden thought in mystic speech.

For us the sun and moonbeams shine,
　　Undoubting faith is still our creed ;
　　And as the same old book we read,
I feel your heart throb close to mine.

Be near me still, and do not break
　　The potent magic of the spell ;
　　If this be life, I love it well,
And if a dream, I would not wake.

THE next morning Percy declared he was much
better, and rose at his usual hour.

"I'm afraid I frightened you last night, Allie," he said, "but there's nothing to be alarmed about. I've lost a little blood, and so of course I feel rather weak, and my head aches more than I care for; so I'll put myself in your hands for a day or two, and then I shall be all right."

At breakfast she thought his manner nervous and unnatural, but he affected to be in high spirits, and talked lightly on many indifferent subjects, carefully excluding from his conversation any reference to the events of the preceding night. Finding him in this mood, Alice endeavoured to reply in the same strain, but was quietly watchful of his movements all the while, and saw, with concern she could not hide, that the energy he had at first displayed was waning rapidly.

"It is no use concealing the truth from me, dear," she said at length, when he had relapsed into moody silence; "you are very ill this morning, and you will be worse if you fatigue yourself by talking."

"Well then, read to me—something light, that doesn't want much effort to follow; I always love to hear your voice."

She gladly complied, for he had not asked her to do this for many months, and it was one of her few accomplishments, which when they were first married, he had constantly praised. After the breakfast things were cleared away, she persuaded him to lie down on the sofa, and having carefully arranged the cushions for his head, she sat by his side, and holding his hand in hers, began to read. She was thus occupied when the doctor who had seen him the night before entered the room, accompanied by an eminent physician.

After a brief examination, they retired to the window for consultation on the case. Although they spoke in low tones, and were at the extreme end of a large apartment, Alice's quick ear caught a few disjointed words, which seemed to her portentous of danger.

" Usual symptoms—inflammation of the brain— may lead to blood poisoning or brain fever. In any case "—

The rest of the sentence was lost.

When the doctors left him, she followed, and leading them to an adjoining room, said firmly—

" I know this is a serious case, but I am quite

ignorant as to the extent of the peril. Tell me the whole truth without any reservation; you need not fear my losing self-control; I have too grave work before me for that."

The younger doctor began some professional platitudes about there being always hope while life lasted, and the patient's advantages of youth and strength; but the physician, after a close scrutiny of her face, terminating in a nod of approval, said briefly, though not unkindly—

"If you are strong, madam, as you say and as you seem—anticipate the worst; it is not absolutely inevitable, but it is most likely."

She had been flushed by excitement before this, but now the colour faded from her face. The deathlike pallor of her cheek showed how deeply his words had moved her, but she bowed calmly, and left the room with a murmured word of apology and thanks.

For three or four days there was little change in Percy's condition, and any slight change there may have been seemed to be for the better. He still complained of headache and giddiness, but the weakness he had at first betrayed was less perceptible.

The only allusion he made to the gamblers was on the fourth day, when he said suddenly—

"Alice is my pocket-book safe?"

"Where is it, Percy?"

"In the breast pocket of the coat I wore the last time I went out."

She left the room to see, but soon returned with the intelligence that she had examined all the pockets thoroughly, and no such thing was there. He did not seem surprised, but there passed a dark look across his face she had never seen before, and he murmured hoarsely—

"Then they have robbed me; I understand their flight now. Curse them!"

"Was there much money in the pocket-book?" Alice asked anxiously, more mindful of the effect upon him than the actual loss.

"More than I care to think of, but it is gone— let the thing drop."

"But will you not take any measures to recover it?"

"It would be useless," he answered wearily; "they have four days start of me— they may be half way to America by this time. I could not trace them, and if I did I could prove nothing. Let it drop, I say; I won't have the thing talked about."

The last words were spoken in so irritable a tone that Alice was afraid to pursue the subject, lest it should unduly excite him.

After this he became moody and abstracted, often sitting for more than an hour without uttering a word.   To the doctors and any of the servants who chanced to enter the room he spoke irritably, but his manner towards Alice grew gentler every day, and he seemed to rely more and more upon her.   She scarcely left his side for a moment, but would talk to him cheerfully when he was strong enough to bear it, read from some favourite book, or sing old ballads in a low voice, as if he had been a child she was seeking to lull to rest.   At other times when she fancied he was weary, she would be perfectly silent, and engage herself with crochet or embroidery, though her attention was never so absorbed in her work that a single want of his (indicated by a restless movement or gesture), although scarcely recognised by himself, escaped her.

Wearied with watching and harassed by anxiety,

these days were yet among the sweetest of her married life, for they proved that he was still dear to her; they softened the bitterness of many lonely musings, they gave her the repeatedly longed for opportunity of serving him, and they drew the two hearts, so unlike in character, though bound by sacred ties, closer together. She knew it instinctively before a word to this effect had passed his lips, but at length he said—

"How good you are, Allie; you must be very tired with all this watching, yet I have not seen an impatient look once pass across your face. I wish I were like you."

"Nonsense," she answered lightly; "you would be patient enough if I were ill."

He shook his head, and was silent for a few minutes; then he resumed—

"I never have been patient in my life—no one can know that better than my poor Allie. Since I have been ill, many things seem confused to me, my head aches, and I feel so weary that I cannot think long on any subject but one. That thought will not leave me, and I understand it now as I never did before."

"What is it, Percy?"

"The consciousness of having wronged you. For the last few days this idea has seemed to throb through my very blood—sometimes a definite thought shaping itself into sternly reproachful words—at others a vague perception, like the consciousness of pain in sleep. It has mingled itself with numberless strange fancies—dreams I should call them, if it were not that all the while I knew I was in my own house, and you, darling, sitting by my side."

"What fancies, Percy?"

"I thought we were children again at Seafern, but not with the old gladness of heart. I was wretched because I knew I had wronged you, and you were miserable because I had made you so. I could not tell what I had robbed you of— some trifling possession, perhaps merely a plaything, but the effect was real enough, and I tried to make restitution, but the scene changed, and you looked as you did when Sydney and I met you on the country road, after my long absence in London. The scene changed, I say, but the old bitterness remained, all the sharper because I read reproach in the eyes of a proud maiden, instead of a child. Then there was another transformation, and I saw what was not fancy, but reality—the promise not given voluntarily, but wrung from you by circumstances—the wedding to whose vows I have been faithful in the letter, but false in spirit—and then the last two years"—

She laid her hand gently on his lips.

"Do not speak of that," she said. "Let us think only of the far-off past, not with these morbid fancies, but with grateful remembrance of happy days. The last two years have had much of sadness in them—we have not been to each other all we might have been ; but you reproach yourself too bitterly—I, too, am not free from blame. Forgive me, and let us turn our eyes towards the future—that is still ours."

"It is yours," he answered, with something of the old lethargy creeping over him. "May it be fair as your own sweet face, darling."

They kissed each other, and he sank back fatigued. Alice brushed the tears hastily from her eyes, conscious at that moment of a pain which had in it an element of exquisite joy.

"He will recover," she thought; "he must be

better, or he would not have been able to frame his thoughts so calmly. He will recover, and the happiness we have never known together may be ours at last."

But that evening he was delirious, and re-enacted incoherently his conversation with her—his accusation of the gambler, and many more remote episodes of his life. This condition with intervals of exhaustion lasted two days: on the third he seemed more collected, and two or three times uttered her name; but when she asked him if he felt stronger, he shook his head. At length by a great effort he half raised himself in the bed, and said faintly—

"Come with me to the cave Allie—it will not be lesson-time for an hour, and we've not been there for days. How fast the tide is going out—see how the waves laugh and leap and sparkle in the sunlight; did you say they were cruel? you are wrong—they are the merriest playfellows . . . how bright it is here! When I am a man Allie, you and I will"—

His voice failed, and he fell backwards quite exhausted. In a little while all was over, and Alice had kissed his cold lips with the sacred tenderness of a last farewell. From that moment her two years of weary wedded life seemed to fade from her memory; and she thought of him once more as the little playfellow, whom long ago she had loved so well.

CHAPTER IX.

Perhaps the wildest enterprise of ancient chivalry was less difficult than the single handed combat with the world, in which heart and brain and hands are the only weapons—in which the prize of triumph is not glory but bread. Yet this is the every-day existence of millions; and opulent common sense watches the struggle with faint interest, rewarding victory with unsolicited tolerance, and defeat with gratuitous censure.

WHEN the old die, although the " troops of friends" of whom Macbeth speaks may weep sincerely, there is little bitterness in their tears. The broken circle had indicated its full meaning— the highest possibilities of the nature had been reached: the life thus ended may have been a poem, a satire, or a calculation; but in any case the greatest thought had been written — the brightest arrow had left the bow string—the result most eagerly sought for, had been ascertained; and by the inexorable law bound up with every fibre of the universe, the warfare passes into more active hands. But it is far otherwise when the veiled messenger of Heaven enters the gay scene where young hearts are throbbing to the subtle harmony and rapid rhythm of hope and love. Then the icy touch seems often wanton and almost always cruel; for our eyes are dim, and the creeping mists of earth hide from us the celestial city which is the goal of pilgrimage.

A fortnight before, Percy had been well and strong, regarding death as a dark heritage of the far-off future: now his handsome boyish features were white and rigid—the clear blue eyes had lost their lustre—the irresolute mouth had become fixed and changeless, by intensity of meaning.

He had had many acquaintances, but few friends. Careless natures like his, open hearted, generous, gay, but without any profound depth of mind or heart, are always popular; but it is not for such as these that men will die, or women bear unsuspected pain—silently and without complaint through lonely years. His father had fostered what was worst in his character, by idolatrous affection which denied him nothing—his friend Sydney Mayfield had believed him endowed with many qualities he could never by any possibility possess; and the little girl who had played with

him on the sands of Seafern, forgot nothing of
their old companionship now she was a woman;
but beyond this there were few, if any, who
thought about him with deeper feeling than passing regret.

Sydney was far away, and knew nothing of all
that had happened; and there was no one to comfort Alice in this moment of unlooked for sorrow
—no one to tell her that her self-reproaching
thoughts were undeserved. She was weary from
the undue strain and terrible anxiety of the last
few days, and probably felt the reaction, from the
longer constraint she had imposed upon herself—
the part she had been compelled to play, and the
mental torture of retrospect and apprehension.

"You are looking feverish and ill Mrs. Fenwood," the doctor said to her, "you have been
overtaxing your strength."

Alice tried to deny this, but soon felt it was too
true.

"I shall be better in a day or two," she said;
but her face belied her words, and the pen she had
taken up with the intention of writing fell from
her hand.

" Do not fatigue yourself," said the doctor. " Is there anything I can do for you? "

" I wish to speak to Mr. Greville," she replied, " he was my husband's solicitor and friend; if I am to be ill, there are some directions I must give him first."

The doctor readily undertook the message, and Mr. Greville accordingly called that evening.

"Are you ill my dear Mrs. Fenwood? " he inquired, after the first words of greeting, "I am afraid all this sorrow has been too heavy a burden for you."

" It may be so; it is the possibility of that which made me send for you. Percy told me that he had made you his executor, and I know you were more in his confidence than any one. You were his father's friend too, and there are circumstances connected with this death, I think you ought to know; and if I postpone telling you even for a week, it may be too late."

Without further prelude she told him what she knew, besides giving him the needful keys and business details he would require for the immediate necessities of administration. It was arranged that he should act with discretionary power in all matters needing prompt attention; and wait until she felt stronger before disposing of the things more nearly affecting herself.

It was many weeks before the time arrived, for Alice suffered at this period from the most serious illness she had ever known; but at length her fine constitution, aided by the careful nursing of a faithful servant, and the efforts of medical skill, triumphed; and she began slowly to recover something of her former strength.

"You are so much better to-day Mrs. Fenwood," the doctor said to her at last, "that I think I may consent to your seeing Mr. Greville to-morrow. He has been worrying me about this interview for days past."

"Has he? If I had known that, doctor, I should have been tempted to disregard your instructions. I am quite well enough to see him to-day; but let it be to-morrow since you wish it."

The solicitor came next morning, and after congratulating her on her recovery, proceeded at once to business.

"From what you told me last time I had the pleasure of seeing you," he said, "I at once in ferred that there were some suspicious circumstances lurking behind your poor husband's midnight adventure. The suspicion became certainty when I discovered that the money paid for the sale of Scafern Hall had disappeared, without any indication being given as to the direction in which it had gone. I found on investigation that the gamblers had vanished too, and of course associating them with the idea of robbery I took prompt measures for their detection. The course ninety-nine out of a hundred men take, when they have managed to get hold of a large sum that isn't their own, is to go at once to America, and I wish the States joy of these exported vagabonds. Well, I traced two men exactly answering the descriptions of Ford and Drummond to Liverpool; and I found that they took their passage by the Ocean Sprite, under assumed names."

"You had no doubt of their identity?" inquired Alice.

"None whatever—it was corroborated in half

a dozen ways. Well, the Ocean Sprite was caught in a storm about the middle of the Atlantic, and went down with every soul on board; so that our hunt came to an abrupt conclusion, and the rogues escaped all further chance of punishment."

Alice thought of Mary Ford with rapid sympathy —she, at least, had had no share in the knavery, except in suffering from its consequences: and Alice determined to find the poor girl out, and do what lay in her power to comfort her.

"There is another matter I wish to speak to you about," continued the lawyer; "but it is a troublesome affair, and as you are not quite strong yet, I had better defer it till some other time."

"No," said Alice quickly, "tell me now, if you please, Mr. Greville—anything is better than suspense."

"Well then, I must tell you that the condition of your husband's estate is very far from satisfactory. Where the money has all gone to, I really don't know—he had fifty thousand pounds two years ago; but when I came to examine affairs first, I feared there would not be more than ten shillings in the pound for the creditors."

Alice looked at him with sudden alarm, not unmingled with incredulity.   Poverty she had often thought of, and not by any means with un-mixed dread; but the possibility of bankruptcy had never crossed her mind.

" You say that was your first impression—then you do not think so now ? " she asked hurriedly.

" No, not altogether.   I challenged every claim —some of them were for debts paid long since, and were effectually settled by being thrown into the waste-paper basket.   Others were monstrously exorbitant, and a few words reduced them by a discount of fifty per cent.   I find too, that the plate and furniture are far more valuable than I expected, and I have very little doubt when they are sold there will be enough to satisfy every claimant.   I tried to get them to accept a sub-stantial composition ; but they are all sharks, and stood by their bonds like so many Shylocks."

Alice's thoughts were too much absorbed by this unlooked-for revelation to suggest to Mr. Greville that his similes were rather entangled.   " I have some valuable jewellery," she said, " let that go too, if there is any necessity for it—it may turn the balance."

" I think it will," said Mr. Greville, touched with

genuine sympathy, though his voice was little altered from its usual dry professional tone. "I am very sorry things should have come to this pass, my dear Mrs. Fenwood; but I am afraid there is no alternative."

"But you said he had originally fifty thousand pounds," she repeated, scarcely able to believe his words. "We have lived extravagantly, I know— I have often told Percy so; but we cannot have spent all that."

"Money takes wings when the gaming-table assists its flight," was the significant reply. "I find the whole system of expenditure to have been far too lavish; but if that had been all, you might have been driven in your carriage for years to come. As it is, the crash was inevitable, and the question not one of years, but of months. I note with special regret that your legacy of three thousand pounds from Mr. Fenwood was never settled upon you, but must go in the universal deluge."

The thoughts which crowded on Alice's mind were not very bright or encouraging in character; avarice is essentially a masculine vice, and she had both the undesirable vagueness of view on money matters and the generous disregard of sordid considerations which are so often seen in her sex. But this announcement of ruin was a rough destruction of preconceived ideas, and made her feel more bitterly that she was alone and friendless in the world. To part with luxury was no great sacrifice, but she had thought of leaving London — of living in some quiet country place with two or three servants that she had known from childhood, and redeeming the tranquil course of her life from common-place by thought for the poor and consecration of her wealth to their needs. Now her first consideration must be how to obtain the commonest necessities for herself; and with this for a primal life-object, the world seemed a dreary vista of effort almost fruitless—cold, sunless, and uninviting.

Still she looked so steadily at Mr. Greville, that he fancied she had not comprehended the full meaning of his words; but when he began to repeat them she stopped him, and said—

"Yes, I understand, Mr. Greville. I wish you had been the bearer of brighter tidings; but regret is idle—or at all events, the expression of it is so.

With regard to the practical issue, I rely wholly on you; must everything be sold?"

" I am afraid so."

" Then let it be as soon as possible—I do not fear poverty, but I do shrink from uncertainty and suspense."

Her wishes were obeyed, and the house was soon besieged by Jews, upholsterers, workmen, old ladies in quest of abnormal bargains, and stray idlers. One small room Alice had reserved for herself, for she had no other home to go to, and until she knew the final results of the sale she could not absolutely decide what course was most advisable for her to take. So she remained in the midst of the noise and confusion hidden from observation; but not so far away as to shut out the sounds of whistling, heavy footsteps, and loud voices. She scarcely heeded them, although more than once she knew, from the frequent mention of her own name, that she and her husband were the subjects under discussion; but she felt it all vaguely, like a murky atmosphere, and was very miserable.

Mr. Greville had tried to persuade her to take

refuge in his own house ; but she was not sure of a welcome from his wife, a lady of somewhat acid disposition, and therefore had declined his offer with many thanks. A few days after Percy's death, Ethel Stafford had written to her cousin with superlative expressions of love and sympathy in every phrase, and all the most tender passages of her letter were freely underlined.

But on her recovery, Alice had sent her a brief reply concisely stating the facts of her illness and ruin ; and to this letter there had been no answer. She naturally inferred, therefore, that with this change in her social position, there had been a corresponding alteration in the ardent attachment of her pretty cousin ; and smiled to think how little human nature has changed since the first satirists wrote about the disinterestedness of friends.

At length the sale ended, and the last purchaser left the house ; and after three days of monotonous quiet, which, dull as it was, Alice felt to be a relief after the recent noise, Mr. Greville appeared with papers in his hands to give her the information she wanted.

"This empty house is very desolate for you, Mrs. Fenwood," he began, "surely you are not living alone here."

"No, I have my faithful nurse still, to whom I owe my life; she will not hear of leaving me until my future is settled. Can you speak more definitely to-day, Mr. Greville?"

"Yes; everything is settled now. The sale has turned out better than I expected on the whole, for when the Jews get the bidding in their own hands things go for next to nothing. I have given all my time and attention to this affair, and under ordinary circumstances should myself have made a heavy claim on the estate. The account may possibly seem high to you as it is; but I assure you I have only charged what was absolutely necessary."

He placed an ominous-looking paper before her as he spoke. She glanced at the total—it was a large amount, but not so much as she had expected.

"I hope this claim can be fully met," she said.

"Oh yes; there are funds enough for that."

"And I trust the trouble you have taken—for

which, believe me, I am sincerely grateful—has not caused you any actual loss."

"No," said the lawyer, half-regretting that he had not struck out a few more items in the account, "I have saved some of your jewels, Mrs. Fenwood —it has not been necessary to part with them all."

Alice looked pleased—"I am very glad of that," she said, "they were Percy's gifts, and to think of them being all sold cost me a pang."

"The money surplus is ridiculously small," resumed Mr. Greville, "only thirty-four pounds. I brought you a cheque for the amount, thinking that you might—might need it."

"I am richer than I thought," said Alice, with a faint smile, as he laid the cheque and jewel-case on the table.

Mr. Greville looked compassionately at her, thinking how young and inexperienced she was, and what rough handling the world might have in store for her.

"Can I serve you in any way?" he asked. "What are your plans?"

"I have scarcely formed any; but I think of

being a governess, or a companion to some lady.
I suppose such a position will not be hard to get."

"Harder than you expect, unless you have
influential friends. Perhaps I can do something
for you—I should be very glad if I could.
You don't care for my wife, or else my own
children want looking after enough, in all conscience."

Alice shook her head with a quiet smile; for
she knew Mr. Greville regarded dislike of his wife,
as a natural and even laudable characteristic.

"Well, I'll think what I can do, and let
you know this evening. You will still be here, I
suppose."

"Yes, certainly, if you wish to see me; but I
have no intention of remaining more than a day
or two," and so he left her.

In the afternoon one of his clerks brought her a
hurried letter, saying he had just been called to
Paris by an old client on most urgent business.
He was sorry not to be able to keep his appointment, but enclosed his address for the next few
weeks, and begged her to write to him if she
needed help of any kind. He added in a post-

script that he had instructed his cashier to honour her drafts to the extent of a hundred pounds—a permission of which he knew she was not likely to avail herself, but a balm to his conscience nevertheless, soothing any unquiet remembrance of that morning's account. The clerk had not been gone many minutes, when there was another loud knock, and while Alice was wondering who else would come to see her, the door was rather abruptly opened, and Mr. Stafford entered the room.

His manner was not so calm as usual, for he seemed actuated by conflicting impulses, and unable to regard anything with his wonted cool decision. At first he was evidently irritable and indignant; but the sight of Alice in her widow's dress—her fair face eloquent of patient suffering, seemed to soften him; and he said not unkindly—

"This is a dismal business; but it is not your fault, and I'm sorry for you—upon my honour I am, but your husband must have been greatly to blame; he ought "—

" We will not speak of him, if you please uncle," interrupted Alice, in a firm tone; " he is beyond the reach of praise or censure now."

"That's true—still business is business, and he must have been confoundedly extravagant. I'll be bound he never gave you the faintest hint that things were coming to this pass."

"I don't think he knew himself."

"That makes matters worse—not better. I can pardon anything under heaven, sooner than imbecility in the common duties of life. If a man can't manage his own affairs, what on earth can he be trusted with? There—I won't pursue the subject since it seems to pain you. Let us be sensible—what do you mean to do?"

"I shall look out at once for a situation as governess or companion."

"Your training has admirably fitted you for it," he said, feeling his indignation rising again; "have you saved nothing from this lamentable wreck?"

She showed him the cheque and her jewel case—

"That is all I have in the world," she said, simply.

Mr. Stafford glanced at both objects with an expression the reverse of encouraging.

"A cheque for thirty four-pounds, a locket, two or three brooches, and a few chains and rings!"

he exclaimed, "that's a hopeful capital to begin life with. What has become of your diamonds?"

"They are sold."

"I thought as much. Has your late husband been made a bankrupt?"

"Do you think I should retain even as much as this if he had?" she demanded, proudly, "the claim of every creditor has been paid in full, and as you were not among their number, uncle, I cannot see what cause you have for being angry with me."

"Bah! that's talking like a woman—I am not angry, and to prove it I will make you a proposal. You talk of being a governess—you have had no experience, so its no use asking what you can teach, for you can't teach anything; but what do you know?"

Alice felt rather stung by this laconic summing up of her capabilities, but as it only affected her-self, thought it best to make no retort.

"I have had a fair English education," she said, "I know the rudiments of French and Italian; and I picked up a very slight smattering of Greek from Mr. Fenwood."

"That won't be any use to you in teaching

girls," was the not too gracious rejoinder, "the
modern languages are all right, if your knowledge
is not half imaginary; but they are matters of
course. Can you teach music ? "

" No."

" Or drawing ? "

"Not at all—I have learned both, but I have
ability for neither."

Mr. Stafford whistled despondently for two or
three minutes.

" You might be a companion," he observed, " to
an irritable valetudinarian, who would make her
nerves the excuse for every kind of petty tyranny; or
you might be a nursery governess, which means
having ten times the work and humiliation of a
nursemaid, with not much more than half the pay.
I said I had a proposal for you—it is this—come
and live with us."

" I will not be dependent on any one," returned
Alice, warmly, " the meanest drudgery would be
better than constant reproaches which unwilling
gratitude would compel me to bear in silence."

"Nonsense dear," he replied more kindly than
he had spoken yet, "I did not know you were so

sensitive, or I would not have talked so freely. You can be as independent in my house, as anywhere else if you like. The governess who taught Nellie and Daisy has just left—why should you not take her place? The salary I gave her was not large—in fact it was only eighteen pounds a year; but "—

" I would not accept any salary from you," said Alice, " but if you will consent to my coming to your house for a month, with the idea of seeing whether I can be of any use or not, I will come."

" Have it your own way, I have no doubt we shall get on well together, Ethel is very fond of you I know, and so are the children. I shall expect you to-morrow."

So next day Alice said farewell—not without tears, to the woman who had known her as a child and lingered by her side with unaltered love and respect, through the vicissitudes of fortune, which had driven so many away. Her few remaining possessions were soon packed, and with a heavy heart she left the desolate house, which a little more than two years before, she had first entered as a bride.

CHAPTER X.

Tho songless forest is brown and bare
To tho bitter scorn of tho chilling air;
Whilo life is heavy and faint with care.

The city is bound with a golden chain,
The crowd has never a hope but gain,
And my heart is weary of lonely pain.

For woods must loso the bloom of May,
Dull greed is blind to the light of day;
And the queen of my soul is far away.

WHEN Sidney Mayfield left England he had no
more definite intention than to escape from haunt-
ing ideas and familiar surroundings, whose altered
aspect had become wearisome to him. To a man
of clear and vigorous intellect, strong feelings and
convictions, and a resolute will, a purposeless life
is intolerable ; but he seemed now to be sailing on
an infinite ocean without a rudder, while the
dreams of love and ambition, which like stars had
guided his course, were lost in impenetrable darkness.

He knew this state of feeling was not wholly

right—that happiness is not the primary object
for which man was sent into the world to strive—
that love is the companion of comparatively few,
while duty follows all like an inexorable shadow :
but abstract truth is cold, and Sidney could not
think calmly of a world in which Alice had for
him no part.

He was not ungenerous in his sorrow, and never
for a moment blamed her. On the contrary, he
treasured every word she had spoken in their last
interview, and found his truest consolation in be-
lieving from this slight evidence, that she had
truly loved him—that she had not been inconstant
or forgetful, that she had only acted in accordance
with her own conviction of duty—mistaken doubtless, yet not the less imperative in its demands.

Nor did he blame Percy : why should he quarrel
with any man for loving what he himself regarded
as the most precious thing on earth ? If he had
viewed his old schoolfellow in the dry light of impartial truth, he might have recognised that such
a love as his own was no more possible to Percy
than the gift of astrological prophecy ; but when
the idea had crossed his mind, he had dismissed

it as petty and unworthy. No man could live with her and not love her, he had thought, and why should he consider himself more fitted for that high honour than another? In one sense too, Percy had a prior claim—he had known her from a child, and his family had had the sweet privilege of befriending her, when she was poor and lonely.

Yet he could not trust himself to meet her in her new home—to see her love for her husband daily deepening, and whatever regard or affection she had once given him, slowly fading from her heart. He could not bear the thought of masking feelings which had obtained complete mastery over him, with an assumption of polite indifference, and in addition to all this, he remembered that she had said it would be better for them never to meet again. He knew his own heart too well to fancy that time could ever bring him its fatal gift of forgetfulness; but in a few years he would be more able to resume the interrupted course of his life—he would be nothing to her then, for in all probability by that time her children would have drawn her closer to her husband, and the last remembrance of a girlish love have been hope-

lessly crushed by baby hands. It was better so,
he thought; since it was a woman's nature to
be unselfishly devoted to those around her, and
cold to those who are far away, it was idle to
quarrel with the inevitable. After all, if the
alternative lay between pain for himself at being
forgotten, or sorrow for her in remembering, he
would unhesitatingly choose the former burden,
heavy as it was; and think it cowardly to re-
sent its weight.

But the test of fortitude lies far less in the
formation of heroic resolve than in the patient
fulfilment of it; and the performance of petty
duties, as well as the endurance of small trials,
would he knew, be a severer strain. He did not
fear the final result even of this, for there was too
much stern strength in his manhood to be crushed
because a bright dream had perished; but he felt
the struggle would be a hard one, and was glad of
any aid which changing scenes could give him.
Before this time he had always loved his work,
and had devoted all his energies and sympathies
to it; but now it seemed poor and useless, and he
dreaded the idea of his degenerating into mere

mechanical execution of a task which had once
been a vocation. Whatever else he lost, he must
recover the healthy tone of his mind; and to do
this, fresh interests, and consequently new reflections, seemed the most potent influences.

He went to Italy, and sought to find the help
and teaching he needed in her ancient treasury of
imaginative wealth; but art requires complete
devotion, and to a mind preoccupied with other
thoughts she speaks obscurely, like a sibyl uttering
a divine message in an unknown tongue. Sydney
soon grew weary of the beauty which in calmer
moments would have been a continual poem and
inspiration to him. Here, too, he met people he
knew, who rarely failed to subject him to exquisite
torture by inquiries concerning his plans for the
future and the probability of his soon returning to
England.

He therefore left the cities and spent the winter
in an obscure village, where an English traveller had
scarcely ever been seen before. Here he was regarded
with wonder, not only by reason of his nationality,
but because to the simple people of the place his
actions were quite incomprehensible. " He must

be a great scholar," they said to each other, "for does not the priest talk to him with respect and submission as to a learned man? He must possess great wealth too, for there is gold in his purse, and he spends it freely; and surely he is kind, for he sent wine to the old woman who was dying, and gives the children money for fruit and toys. But he is always grave—he takes long and solitary walks, and when he passes Beatrice Solani, our fairest maiden, she smiles at him but he never seems to see."

When the spring came he left Italy for Switzerland, choosing as before the least frequented places, where his income would not only be equal to his simple wants but leave him some small surplus for helping others. Solitude is a dangerous refuge for a morbid nature, but Sydney was young and strong, with perceptions that were generally instinctively true; and before many months he felt that life, even in its altered aspect, was not robbed of all brightness and colour—he could not live among the mountains, and cherish egotistic conceptions of the universe; he could not dwell in constant companionship with nature and be unmindful of her loveliness; he could not see the manifold possibilities of work which existed wherever men and women were found and be ungrateful. He studied, too, more steadily than his busy life had hitherto given him the opportunity of doing since he left school; and if the pleasures in the broad world of literature are calmer and less brilliant in hue than the delights of action, when the hot blood flows with exultant passion from a young heart, they are more constant and enduring.

In his wanderings he did not become cynical or hopeless, but everywhere he found something lacking, and his dearest enjoyment was shadowed by the sense of incompleteness. The objects around him were strange and beautiful, but he could not give them undivided attention, for the thought of Alice was with him always; and he could not banish from his mind the remembrance of their parting when he had read in her eyes infinite possibilities that could never be fulfilled.

At length he began to long for the larger life of towns, for something like familiar scenes—for the sound of English-speaking voices. This impulse being strong upon him, and the disinclination to re-visit England not having disappeared, he determined to cross the Atlantic and see something of the New World.

In America he found much to interest and amuse him, as all men must do who view that strange great country from any standpoint but that of political prejudice. Transatlantic society is not poetical—it lacks the serene beauty of tradition, its precocious activity has not been tempered by wise moderation, and its popular thought painfully lacks the truest of all emotions—reverence. But there is much that is noble in its spirit of freedom and enterprise which Englishmen are prone to overlook in their just hatred of reckless speculation, bubble companies, and stump oratory, as well as their views being strongly tinctured by undue familiarity with the grotesque side of the national character.

Sydney was much impressed by the general earnestness: the object pursued might not always be a worthy one, nor the means by which it was to be attained wholly free from objection; but indolence had no place here, and the necessity of once more taking his part not as a spectator of

active life, but as a sharer in it, was continually
forced upon him. Something too, of the universal
passion of restlessness seemed to have seized him,
for he visited one great city after another without
making a long stay at any. The wild extent and
rugged beauty of American scenery spoke in deeper
tones, and when at length he left Niagara—that
monarch of cataracts, whose aspect seems to
embrace every gradation of beauty from the lightest
and most delicate to the majestic and sublime,
whose unceasing voice is Nature's organ music,
more eloquent in its teaching of God's eternity
than all the volumes of theology that have ever
been written—the unrest of heart and mind with
which he had started on his wanderings was
silenced, if not calmed.

In Toronto, he seemed to have been suddenly
transported back again to England, with only occasional reminders that he was still far away—for
perhaps nowhere on the great American continent
are English ideas so prominent as in this part of
Western Canada; and notwithstanding its wooden
pavements, and its numerous houses of the same
material, it is only when the city is known

familiarly that the illusion disappears. He did not stay long here, but went by the Grand Trunk Railway to Montreal, arriving there in the autumn —the fall, as it is called, when Nature's mood is most liberal, as friends are wont to be before a long farewell; when the hot summer is ended, and the cruel winter has not commenced; when the days are brilliant with sunshine, and the crimson wonders of sunset deepen into the serener loveliness of moonlight nights. In this part of Canada there is a strange blending of French and English ideas, which is evidenced even by the hum of conversation in the streets and railway trains, where the rough voices of Englishmen, and the nasal tones of the Yankees, or Canadians who have been much in the States, alternate with the rapid utterance of the *patois*, which in Montreal and Quebec is called French.

One evening two or three weeks after he came to the city, Sydney was walking through the Mount Royal Cemetery when his attention was arrested by the attitude and face of a woman kneeling in the Roman Catholic part beside a carefully tended grave. Perhaps it was merely the current of his thoughts which gave him the idea, but in some vague way she reminded him of Alice. She was not so tall, and in place of the luxuriant beauty he knew so well, and the cheek flushed with the activity of youthful health, was a woman slight and delicate, whose pale face showed that the loveliness she had once possessed had faded years before. She was probably not more than thirty, but the beauty of French-Canadian women is swift both to ripen and decay.

As he approached her, she rose and left the grave, on which she had deposited some exquisite flowers. The path they had each to tread was a narrow one, and as Sydney stood aside to let her pass his nearer view of her face increased rather than diminished his curiosity. He felt strongly inclined to speak to her, but respect for the sanctity of grief silenced him, and he passed her with merely a grave inclination of the head. He had not walked many yards, however, before he saw on the ground a little gold cross, and at once concluding it must be hers, hurried after her with it. She took it from him with a smile and word of thanks, saying, with a finer accent than is commonly spoken among the poorer class of the city, to which by her simple black dress she seemed to belong—

"You are very good, monsieur, and I am grateful. This little cross is to me most precious—I should have been desolate without it."

They stood together on the hillside, the soft light of the sunset falling on her face, and Sydney no longer doubted whether she had once been beautiful. As she spoke the last words, with the pretty exaggeration of her race, she gazed at the calm blue waters of the St. Lawrence flowing far beneath, with the same singular expression he had noticed before.

"I thought it might be so," he said, finding she was not averse to being spoken to, "I fancied it might be the gift of some dear friend."

He saw she trembled as she answered—

"It is even so—it was given me by my dearest of friends—my only friend—my love who sleeps silently in yonder grave."

"I fear I have pained you by my words," he said with quick delicacy, but she replied simply—

"No monsieur, it is the most great joy of life

to think of him, and to speak of him is always
sweet. But my history, though it is all the
world to me, is nothing to you—I will not weary
you to hear it."

"I should not be wearied, if to tell it would
not pain you."

"You are kind—I saw that in your face from
the first moment. Listen then, it is a poor tale
—love and sorrow—that is all. My father was a
woodcutter, and my mother died when I was born.
My father's work called him away to Manitoba—
he could not take me with him, baby that I was,
so he left me here in Morraiarle " (the French
Canadian's pronunciation of the word Montreal
is more rapid and delicate than this orthography
would suggest; but perhaps no other letters can
more accurately convey an idea of the sound.)
"He paid a few cents a week to a family for my
board : they were poor, and made me feel daily
that I was little profit to them. They were not
kind to me, and I often wonder how I lived on
their scanty fare; but I was not miserable, for
the sun shines brightly in Morraiarle you know,
and there were many children poor and ragged

like myself to play with, so that sometimes I was
almost happy. But when I was thirteen my
father died, and the people where I lived kept me
for a servant. I know not how long this lasted—
not many months I think; but time passes slowly
when you are wretched, and there was for me
labour and weariness but no joy. I was young
and foolish, but I worked hard—yes very hard;
but they blamed me for being idle, and half-
starved me; but at last there came a change."

"It is her eyes that remind me of Alice,"
Sydney thought, as he saw how the last remembrance seemed to thrill her with triumphant joy;
but he did not interrupt her, and she resumed—

"I say there came a change, for the good God
does not let us weep for ever, He is too merciful
for that. One day the woman at whose house I
lived, was ill; and a young doctor came to see
her. He was an Englishman, and of him I had
heard before—that he was learned, and good, and
kind, caring more for the poor who could not pay
him, than the rich who lived in the houses gay
and great. When he saw me he seemed interested, and asked me questions. I told him all

my story, for we were alone, and begged him to
help me. He asked me what I wanted, and I told
him to go to school like other girls, and be spoken
to in the gentle tone. He said, 'I am not rich
Jeanette, but I will do what I can.' So he spoke
to the old woman about me, she was grateful to
him for having saved her life, and cared not at all
for me, so she told him he might do with the girl
as he pleased."

It was evident she had almost forgotten Sydney
in the intensity of her feeling; and the animation
of her face, suggested the idea that she was
describing what she saw, rather than recalling a
memory.

"So the whole world changed, and grew in a
moment soft and bright. Every one was kind
now—I was well-dressed, well-fed, and taught all
the things I had wished to know—yes, and many
more besides. I was quick to learn, and I worked
hard for his sake. Often he came to see me, and
would praise my diligence; so four years passed
by, and one morning I heard one of the girls
whisper to another that I grew more beautiful
every day. I had scarcely thought of that, it is

strange that it should be so in a woman, you will
say; but I was only seventeen, and had a remembrance too vivid of the old days for girlish
vanity. Now I thought if it is as they say, perhaps *he* will notice it too; and this was sweeter
than all other happiness, for I loved him with
passion the most great, with the worship that
could never alter."

Again she paused to recover her self-control:
it was notable that her English was rarely incor-
rect except when she was under the influence of
strong feeling; and then it seemed as if with
thought of bygone days came unconsciously, some
touch of a diction that had once been habitual.

"I wished and longed, but I did not dare to hope.
What was I that he should care for me? And
when one day he said to me, 'There is nothing
in all the world so beautiful as my Jeanette,
darling I love you, be my wife;' the joy seemed
too great to bear. Yes monsieur, we were married, and in Morraiarle where I had wandered a
ragged child, I now lived as a lady, in a large
house. He was not rich, he was too generous
with time and money for that; but we had

enough, and we loved each other. Oh! it was a gay world then—the skies can never be so blue again : I have heard the priests say we are never satisfied with any wealth; but it is not so. I had no wish that was not gratified—had I not my husband and my child? But at last sorrow came, there was a terrible fever throughout the city, and my little one – mon pauvre petit enfant—died. I had not thought I could suffer so much, while he was still with me, but my heart ached bitterly for the baby who had smiled at me with eyes like his. I said 'Let us go away together for the love of God, far from the breath of this cruel fever,' but he answered—'My duty is here Jeanette, would you have other mothers lose their children, and no hand be stretched out to help them?' And so monsieur, the terrible time came, the fever seized him, and I most desolate and weak of heart was left alone."

Throughout her narration her tears had been falling fast, and now she buried her face in her hands and sobbed with the wild excitability of utter grief. At length she controlled her feelings by a strong effort, and said more calmly—

"There is no more to tell, monsieur; he sleeps yonder and my cries are useless, for he does not hear them, though once a tear of mine would have roused all his compassion for me and indignation at those who had made me weep. Mine is a woman's story, not rare, and it all happened ten years ago; but love is deathless, and remembrance eternal—it is only grief that dies."

"And has your grief died?" asked Sydney, struck by the contrast between the calmness of her last words and her former abandonment of sorrow.

She shook her head—"There is a golden city beyond the sunset," she said, "and the good God will let us meet again some day. Meanwhile, I am patient—I have learned to wait."

The words of sympathy and consolation Sydney was about to utter died upon his lips, for there was a strength in the last phrases which told him plainly that the battle had been fought long since, and that she was more fitted to be his teacher than his pupil. "I am patient—I have learnt to wait," he repeated to himself, as he watched her slowly descending the hill in the direction of the

city, " how hard that lesson is to learn ; but the
world is never weary of repeating it, and without
this strength life is a burden too heavy to be
borne."

CHAPTER XI.

" The time draws near the birth of Christ,
 The moon is hid, the night is still ;
 The Christmas bells from hill to hill
Answer each other in the mist.

" This year I slept and woke with pain,
 I almost wish'd no more to wake,
 And that my hold on life would break
Before I heard those bells again."

       TENNYSON.

WITH the rapidity of transition which characterises Canadian seasons the autumn passed away, and on every side Montreal teemed with indications that the stern winter had actually commenced. To Sydney it seemed as if the enchantress (who of old converted the kingdom of the Black Isles into a diminutive pond, and the citizens into four kinds of fish, retaining no more of their humanity than a taste for obscure declamation) had once again pronounced the words of metamorphosis, and that the counteracting influence of some benignant genie had stopped the transformation when it was only half accomplished. A little while before, the air had possessed the languid beauty of the Indian summer—the forests had been a blaze of gold and crimson which no artist's tints could accurately portray, since their lustre seemed to mirror the celestial glories of an evening sky; the rivers (notably the broad St. Lawrence) had flowed with exultant pride of power. Now all was changed—the dreams of fairyland were rudely dispelled, cold winds were bleak and cutting, the trees desolate and leafless, and the mighty rivers bound by icy chains.

Yet although the thermometer registers a coldness of temperature appalling to the English mind, winter in Canada is not the dreary thing it is in milder latitudes; for fog, and its attendant evils of asthma and bronchitis, are all but unknown in the province of Quebec—the sky, when the snow is not falling, or about to fall, retains its azure clearness, like a friend faithful through adversity; and the cold air is not unkindly to the bold and strong, seeming rather like a rough playfellow, who knows his freaks will only exhilarate the energy and make the blood flow with fresh freedom and power. Such weather seems to be

Nature's challenge for men to emulate her activity by skating; and in the enjoyment of that graceful and fascinating art he must be dull indeed who feels nothing of the sense of joy in mere existence, which modern life, by its crowded cities, feverish pursuit of gold, and disdain of athletic cultivation, tends towards making an obsolete emotion, believed in—if not rejected altogether—on no more substantial ground than mere tradition.

But a heavy snowstorm soon made open-air skating an impossibility, and on Christmas Day Sydney, who had felt his whole mental, moral, and physical system braced by the crisp chill air, experienced the sensation of a reaction, which generally succeeds to the enjoyment of high spirits, as he watched how the dimensions of the long drifts were augmented by the large flakes of persistently falling snow.

"No more skating for the present," he said to himself, "and Christmas is scarcely the time one would choose for being alone in a Canadian hotel, with the snow two or three feet deep on the ground already and the clouds looking as if the storm would go on for ever. Last year I was in

Italy, finding it hard to believe it was not an English midsummer. I wonder where I shall be when the twenty-fifth of December comes round again. I wish I could shake off this weariness of spirit—I thought I had gained more control over myself than to let my moods play the part of a barometer, rising or falling with every change in the weather."

He threw himself into an easy-chair by the fireside, and fixing his eyes upon the glowing coals seemed to behold all the familiar scenes there as in an enchanted mirror. An ordinary English fire is quite powerless to cope with the intense cold of a Canadian winter, and the temperature is only made endurable by double doors, double windows, and the systematic heating of the houses by some more effectual apparatus; but it may be questioned whether the mind of any man was ever so abnormally constructed as to find companionship in a stove pipe, and in most houses the open fires burn brightly on the hearth that so important an element of social enjoyment may not be wanting.

The poets have not told us half enough about the sacred flames which gleam with soft light and

generous warmth in our English homes; yet when
we wander through the art galleries of our memory,
we find them to have been the centres of the scenes
when the cup of life was filled with the richest
wine of gladness and content. How the firelight
loved to play sweet freaks of masquerade with
fair faces—to glitter on the shining wealth of
golden hair; to show how poor a thing it was in
comparison with the deeper light of loving eyes;
in a word, how inseparably it was associated with
the idea of home, and all the gladness, pathos,
laughter, tears, and earnest thought which are
bound up with that richest of Anglo-Saxon words.

But when one is alone—when the companions of
other days are isolated from us by distance, or
by death—when the object of life is no longer to
enjoy, but to endure, the burning coals are
sympathetic still, and their companionship
possesses yet deeper meaning. The boisterous
merriment of the leaping flames has gone, but in
the silent depth of the glowing heat are painted
wondrous pictures of cherished retrospect.

It was no new experience for Sydney to sit alone
with such thoughts as these, for his life had been

for the most part a comparatively friendless one; and although the bias of his character was far more inclined towards action than introspection, the necessity in every true man's nature for love and friendship can only cease with the petrifaction of the heart. His reflections now started from various points and wandered through contrasting roads, but they ended always in one destination—the remembrance of the girl he loved: whose heart had for a moment beaten against his own; whose lips had touched his immediately after they had pronounced the hard decision, that it would be better for them never to meet again. He thought of his young mother, whose face he only knew in dreams—of the friend whose champion he had been at school—of the numerous acquaintances who had played parts more or less important in the drama of his later life; but these images followed each other in swift succession, only to give place to the fair form of Alice Easton, facing him as the reality had done when they had rowed together on the lonely sea.

"I am growing a mere dreamer," he said at last, abruptly disturbing his reverie; "I thought my travels had taught me something, but the old longings are as tyrannical as ever. I cannot forget, nor do I crave for that easy remedy of shallow souls; but that girl I saw kneeling by her husband's grave was right: I must be patient—I must learn to wait."

A few weeks later he was walking rapidly down St. James' Street, when just as he reached the Jesuit Church, he heard his own name called, and looking round recognised an old schoolfellow and friend. Whether in his present mood he would have avoided him, had such a thing been possible, is doubtful; for on the one hand he was anxious to escape observation, and on the other he longed to hear something of old companions, from whom he had now been separated for two years. But the alternative of choice was not given him; so he did not attempt to check the instinctive gladness one invariably feels at meeting a familiar face, when one is far away from home.

"Of all men in the world, I think, I least expected to see you Blackburn," he said, as the other clasped his hand, "I thought no inducement would tempt you to brave a sea voyage."

"As for that, necessity does not tempt—it

compels: I have as good a right to surprise as you—I thought you were in Italy, studying art, and accumulating information that would astonish the natives when you returned home."

" I was there some time, but you have ocular demonstration of the fact that I am not there now; but Montreal is not exactly the city for a long conversation in the streets—it would be inconvenient to be frozen in the middle of an epigram; when will you come to my hotel for the discussion of old times, and your favourite Manillas?"

" Mayfield you have an objectionable habit of anticipating one's own thoughts. I am persuaded that if you had been silent a little longer, most of your best remarks would have occurred to me. I was just on the point of asking when you'd come to *my* hotel."

"I will consider the question asked, and my reply is, that it shall be as soon as you like after you have come to see me. Have you any engagement this evening?"

" No."

" Then I shall expect you to dinner at half-past

six—that is the address. If you fail you may expect me to take terrible revenge. I don't know if any assassins are to be hired in this place on moderate terms—I am afraid the air is too cold for that, though some of the rougher kind among the French Canadians, look capable of anything. There is something magnetic about you Blackburn—it is impossible to be five minutes in your society without talking nonsense. Muse over the probable cause of this, and the cheerful prospect of an untimely end, until we meet this evening."

Ernest Blackburn did not fail to keep his appointment; and after dinner he entertained Sydney with an amusing account of all that had happened in the small world of their common acquaintances, until the time he left England three months before. A story of this kind rarely fails to be interesting, for the most monotonous life has its occasional vicissitudes, and when one knows the actors in a drama, it is not absolutely necessary that the plot of the play should be a complicated one. Sydney's sympathy however, was somewhat weakened by his impatience, as Ernest Blackburn talked of engagements, marriages, triumphs, accidents, failures, and deaths, without once mentioning the names that were oftenest in his thoughts. At last he said, unable to repress his feelings any longer—

"Have you seen anything lately of Percy Fenwood? He and I were inseparable once."

"Of course you were—I had forgotten that. How you used to stand up for him whether he was in the right or wrong! If there were such things as school archives, the thrashing you gave Mudson would be handed down to remote posterity. I wonder what's become of that fellow— he was an ill-conditioned vagabond—I must ask a man I know, who always reads the police news if he has heard anything about him."

"You have not answered my question."

"No, to be sure—I haven't much to tell, and that little I daresay you've heard already. You know he's married?"

"Yes."

"Well, your old friend and pupil showed admirable taste—I must do him justice there. His wife is a tall queenly girl, with brown eyes and hair, a perfect figure, and a voice that more than once made me forget the meaning of her words, in admiration of the unconscious music with which she uttered them."

"I have seen her," interrupted Sydney, rather irritated at the careless chatter of his companion.

"Then my sketch in outline need not be shaded —you will recognise its fidelity as it is. Yes, she is very handsome, poor girl, and if only she had been single, I won't say "—

"Why do you call her poor?"

Sydney spoke in a sharp imperative voice; for the mere suggestion that any one should dare to pity her, had swept away his assumption of cool indifference. Ernest Blackburn looked surprised at this altered tone, but merely replied—

"Have you had no correspondence at all with England? I thought you would be sure to know, for it isn't a secret. There is nothing to be read in her fair proud face to corroborate what I say, for she is mistress even of her looks; but I don't fancy a young wife can be very happy, when her husband is going to the dogs at a pace little short of electric."

"What do you mean?"

" Being an unimaginative and prosaic individual
I mean simply what I say. Fenwood has taken
up with a bad set—I don't think he drinks, but
I know he plays recklessly, and for a fellow like
that, gambling can only have one termination."

"Are you certain of this? "

" Of course I am, or I shouldn't have said a
word about it. When they were first married,
they were always giving parties : capital wine he
had in his cellar too, but this season I hear their
house has been as quiet as a cloister. I have
spoken to men who've played with him, and they
tell me that gambling has taken such strong hold
upon him, that he can't by any possibility be
stopped—it's a mere question of time."

Sydney changed the subject by a strong effort,
and contrived to talk on general topics with toler-
able composure, until his companion's departure ;
but when he was once more alone, he sat down to
think of these bitter tidings, with an acute pain
aggravated by the sense of impotence.

He had thought of almost every contingency
but this—he had fancied that there might be between Percy and Alice that shadow more or less

defined, which is inseparable from incompatibility of disposition — he had recognised his boyish friend's inability to sound the sweet depths of her character—he had foreseen the probability of her girlish instinct of hero-worship being starved or thwarted; but the idea of her misery had never crossed his mind. To feel that the prize it had been his dearest ambition to win was gained by another seemed hard enough; but the sharpness of his disappointment was intensified by the knowledge that his rival valued the possession lightly; and neglected it for the gratification of base and sordid passion.

At first, thoughts of anger and resentment crowded on his mind—he had not forgotten old friendship, nor was he disloyal to school companionship; but the stronger love extinguished the weaker, as the noonday sun makes flickering gaslight dim and faint.

" I could have borne any wrong directed against myself," he thought, "and freely have forgiven him for the sake of old days, but that he should cloud her beauty with sorrow, when the sacred trust of her happiness was committed to him is no petty transgression to be lightly condoned," and there rose before him the image of the woman he loved, alone and desolate—her husband unconscious of the grief from which her slighted lover would have died to save her.

But it was not long before the practical character of his mind asserted itself, and he began eagerly to consider if nothing could be done to prevent this cloudy horizon from growing darker. Between husband and wife no intercession was possible—the fetters of wedded life were voluntarily clasped, and however heavy their burden or keen their power to wound, they must be worn to the bitter end; but if he were in England, could he do nothing to arrest Percy's progress in this mad course of dissipation? He believed in the almost infinite power of influence possessed by a strong will; and although only two years older than his former schoolfellow, he had never before asserted a firm conviction or a deliberate intention, without his companion's ultimate submission to it.

"I will go home at once," he said resolutely, "after all there is something cowardly in this eva-

sion of pain; and it is time my desultory ram-
blings should end their purposeless existence. I
will wake him from this fatal dream—I will tell
him he is breaking her heart, and destroying all
that is noble in himself. Poor boy—it cannot be
two years yet since this madness began, and if he
retains anything of his old character, he will
listen to me. Rumour is a lying herald, and it
may not be so bad after all—I'm sorry I thought
so hardly of him; but I'll go home."

His mind was already recovering hopefulness
and strength, for action is the most certain anti-
dote to morbid thought. Moreover, Coleridge
spoke truly and with clearer energy than was
habitual to his mystic intellect, (rendered cloudier
by dreams begotten of indolence and opium),
when he said that—

"To be wroth with one we love
Doth work like madness in the brain,"

and with this more charitable judgment of Percy's
conduct in the past, came new hope as to the possibilities of the future.

His arrangements for departure were soon made
—his hotel bills settled—a hasty note written to

Ernest Blackburn, to the effect that circumstances involved his immediate return to England; and consequently made their further meeting impracticable—his luggage was summarily packed, and he stood in the railway station, trying to realize that he would so soon be again among the scenes from which he had fancied himself exiled for years. He heard the guard's cry—" All on board going East " (a nautical metaphor in which American officials appear to find great delight) and in a few minutes Montreal was out of sight.

Travelling in the provinces of Ontario or Quebec is never very enjoyable—the roads are rough and uneven—the progress of the cars noisy and tedious—the scenery for the most part rugged without grandeur, and wild without being picturesque; but perhaps its depressing character is never more keenly felt, than when the thermometer registers a temperature some degrees below zero; and the wind is blowing with a bitterness recalling Lear's words, and revealing at once the full shame of human treachery, and the disagreeable aptness of the discrowned monarch's illustration. Sydney tried to withstand the depressing influence of his surroundings in vain: sitting opposite to him was an American family, whose proximity would have been more agreeable if the father had indulged with greater moderation in the national pastime of chewing tobacco—if the mother's dress had been less vivid—if the eldest daughter (a decidedly pretty girl of nineteen) had possessed a more musical voice; and the youngest child had expiated the sin of her aggressive precocity, by immolating herself on the altar of some heathen deity. Near them sat an elderly couple evidently from London, who were quarrelling about the probable fate of a missing parcel, with equal disregard to each other's feelings, the observation of their fellow-travellers, and the orthodox functions of the letter H. Two or three old gentlemen were snoring audibly, and the other passengers seemed to be in possession of only infinitesimal individuality.

Sydney tried to turn the current of his thoughts by looking out of the window, but the prospect was not enlivening. They were then passing half-cleared fields, where the tall trees had been felled, and attempts made to destroy the lingering vitality of the stumps by fire. The charred wood presented a grimy contrast to the monotonous whiteness of the snow, and robbed its cold beauty of artistic effect: the winter had set its icy seal on everything, and all vegetation seemed dead.

Sydney shut his eyes, and thought of Alice: these reflections suggested fairer images. Sad they might be, but never wearying or dull, on the contrary, there was a beauty even in their pain, and in connection with these mental pictures, the jolting of the heavy train became a musical reminder that its progress was towards home.

CHAPTER XII.

Ay, this is England but no longer home,
For absent years have severed us like foes ;
And every object wears an altered look.
My friend lies cold beneath the churchyard grass—
And *she* is here no more.

FIFTY years ago a sea voyage had still an element
of novelty and mystery attaching to it, and consequently merited a detailed description ; but now
that distance is everywhere traversed by the swift
feet of electricity, and oceans are crossed by the
most indolent tourists as a matter of course, such
a proceeding would be as superfluous as to publish
a volume of travels in Oxford Street, or minutely
to specify the objects to be seen from Westminster
Bridge. He must indeed, be an enthusiastic
worshipper of colour who does not soon grow
weary of the endless prospect of sea and sky, the
contemplation of which is commonly diluted by
small talk and trivial amusements.

Homeward bound ships are generally less interesting than the same vessels on their outward

course : the passengers are usually fewer and less inclined to be communicative; moreover, if as it happened to Sydney, the voyage is taken in the winter they generally become more or less victims to northern moroseness, chilblains, and other depressing influences of cold.

Still, had his own reflections been of a brighter hue Sydney would not have found life on the good ship Bohemian altogether unamusing; for the deck and the saloon form so limited a world that intercourse almost invariably tends towards confidence, and the study of character ceases to be the blindfold pursuit it so often becomes among the veiled and masked hearts of society. As it was, however, he was in no mood to take a deeply sympathetic interest in strangers, and did not suffer courtesy to ripen into friendship with any of his fellow-passengers.

He had not very extensive opportunities of choice, for the cold and cheerless weather had repelled many of the people, who were beginning to cast wistful glances in the homeward direction, constraining them to endure exile a little longer, and half the state rooms were consequently empty.

Whether the complacent designation of "state-room," by the way, was originally intended as a satire on courts and high officials may be doubted; but it seems probable that the little sleeping cabins were first so called by a disloyal chancery suitor on account of their exquisite discomfort, and the delight with which they are quitted at length by their much-enduring and long-suffering inmates.

Of the few people who were on board little need be said. There was a hypochondriacal dandy, whose attention was pretty equally divided between consternation at the supposed condition of his lungs and anxiety as to the impressive state of his snowy wristbands. There was a youth with a deep voice, sunken eyes, and an abstracted manner, who announced an hour or two after his arrival that he was a poet; but this ingenuous child of song had no opportunity of justifying his claims to that title or perpetrating fresh lyrical atrocities, for he was speedily reduced to an abject condition of hopeless sea-sickness, and confined his romantic indications to the utterance of monotonous and heart-rending groans. There was a pretty coquette of nineteen, who occasioned

several young gentlemen alternate moments
of delirious delight and longer periods of
dark despair. This artless maiden lavished
caresses (with a tenderness the youngest of her
admirers thought absolutely maddening) on a lady
who was travelling with her. This object of envy,
who was a few years older, made strenuous efforts
to appear amiable and fascinating ; and it must be
admitted that in neither case was perseverance
crowned with success. There was a stout lady
with four children, notoriously spoiled, whose
playful freaks made every male creature on board
their deadly enemy—who tyrannised over a nursery
governess with vicious pertinacity, and incurred
no maternal reprobation when they deliberately
tore the poor girl's dress, pulled her hair, or in
other winning ways proved the truth of Words-
worth's assertion, that "Heaven lies about us in
our infancy."

Sydney was fond of children as a rule, but he
felt no temptation whatever to interfere when the
youngest cherub, after numerous exhibitions of this
kind, received condign punishment from the hands
of one of the before-mentioned young gentlemen

who were in love with the belle of the vessel. This was not an action of disinterested justice, but an indignant protest against the youthful pastime of pouring soap and water on the passengers' beds. The stout lady loudly resented any criticism of her darling's conduct; but the infuriated youth was desperate—it was bad enough he probably considered, to wet one's pillow with tears of unrequited passion, without this further introduction of depressing damp.

There was also a deaf old lady who persisted in the belief that her hearing was both acute and delicate, and consequently made most ludicrous mistakes in her conversation—replying to a polite platitude on the subject of the weather with an acquiescent expression of dislike to the present dresses of young girls, and the general depravity of modern times; or answering an inquiry as to her health by some allusion to the wedding attire of her grandmother, as depicted in a painting by a celebrated artist. The remainder of the passengers need not be individually described: they were for the most part commercial men, travelling on business, who formed a society of their own, spoke in terms incomprehensible to the uninitiated, of rising shares and falling markets, and were occasionally boastful touching the resources of their wine cellars and their intimacy with renowned capitalists.

At length the frequent inquiries as to what day they should probably arrive in Liverpool, became more easily answered questions concerning the hour they would land. As Sydney sprang on shore he felt the sense of relief at recovered freedom and the gladness to be at home once more, somewhat shadowed by the dismal appearance of the scene. The Englishman's love of his native country is not an unreasoning patriotism, for in addition to her wealth of history, tradition, and existing heroism, she has a fair face; but to justly note her beauty it must be watched in all moods, and superficial observation of it will generally be wrong.

For the last two years Sydney had been accustomed to the azure loveliness of cloudless skies, and he could not repress a shiver as he saw how the heavy fog and drizzling rain conspired to make the somewhat grimy aspect of Liverpool still less-inviting. It seemed like an ill omen of failure in what he was about to attempt, and as he looked for better encouragement in the faces of the people thronging round him he met with little more success. An emigrant vessel was just starting, and the sight of wives and mothers weeping at a farewell that may be for ever, and must be for weary years, may silence the selfishness of personal grief, but is scarcely a cheerful antithesis to the damp and fog of a February morning.

" Cab, sir—drive you to the 'otel ? " was exclaimed by many voices when his luggage had passed through the ordeal of custom house inspection, and his honourable intentions with regard to Her Majesty's revenue were sufficiently established.

" No," said Sydney, " I'm going to London."

"Carry yer boxes up to the station then, sir ? " This from an augmented chorus.

No further opposition being offered, the luggage was promptly seized and prodigious feats of strength performed with it, in accordance with the invariable custom of the Liverpool porter, who has so long handled heavy weights with ease that he would esteem it beneath his dignity to betray anything remotely resembling care, either for their burden or the safety of their contents.

It was still comparatively early when Sydney reached London, and after booking his luggage he went into the station restaurant with the intention of hastily lunching and then proceeding at once with the matter he had in hand. He was somewhat delayed, however, by the youth who has been already alluded to in connection with the juvenile pleasantry of the soap and water. This gentleman poured into Sydney's ears an account of his distressed affections, and asked him darkly what were his views on the subject of suicide. To this Sydney gave the laconic rejoinder, that he considered a man guilty of such an action was usually both a coward and a fool, which unexpected opinion appeared to make a deep impression on the mind of the young gentleman. He shook Sydney warmly by the hand, and after pensively pledging the queen of his fancy in more glasses of champagne than a temperance advocate would consider strictly advisable he evinced symptoms of conviviality, and philosophically remarked that after all there were many other girls who were very fond of him indeed. In this mood Sydney left him, and hurried on in the direction of the house where Blackburn had told him that Percy lived.

In taking this precipitous course he was actuated by several motives. His object for being in London was almost entirely on Percy's account; if he found all his endeavours to influence him were hopeless, it might be advisable again to leave London for a while, and in that case he would prefer that the fact of his having been there at all should not be known. He rather dreaded the interview, and could not feel quite certain of his self-control in the event of a meeting with Alice; but since neither contingency could be evaded, it would be better to brave them at once and end the uncertainty and suspense which had for the last three weeks been torturing him.

What he wished was to see Percy and arrange some place of meeting where there would be no fear of their conversation being disturbed : the easiest way to do this was to call at his house, and the fact of his having come direct from the ship would be sufficient apology for his refusing the hospitable invitation to stay he knew he should receive, on the ground of fatigue.

He took a cab (a rather unusual practice for him, who, generous almost to extravagance when others were concerned, was obliged to be very sparing in his personal expenditure) and gave the driver the direction, telling him to use his best speed.

As he drove through the familiar streets, he felt his usual calmness quite forsake him in the whirl of excited anticipation. Would his plan succeed and the necessary appointment be made in a few minutes; or would the interview end in his seeing *her?* Had she altered since their last meeting, and did she retain any remembrance of it? Would she calmly ignore the past, and meet him with courtesy merely; or would any inflection of voice, or nervousness of manner betray that she also had not forgotten? Doubts of this kind passed through his mind in rapid succession until the mistrust of his own firmness almost grew into a disinclination to persevere in his intention.

This momentary indecision he conquered as

weak and foolish; but on reaching the corner of
the street where Percy lived, he paid the cabman
and dismissed him. It would be easier for him to
be unnoticed, he thought, if he walked the remainder of the way; and although the rain and
mist were scarcely agreeable, the distance was not
great. He glanced at the monotonous line of
stately houses, built in the dreary style which
characterises the West End of London, and could
not repress a feeling of professional contempt for
the architects who had perpetrated these enor-
mities. "A strange sphere for her to live in," he
thought. "I always associate her with June sunshine and golden waves, and "—

His reflections were unexpectedly interrupted by
his arrival at the house, where the first object
that arrested his attention was a large bill in the
window intimating that this most desirable of
mansions was to let. At first he thought he must
have mistaken the number, but this he found on
looking at his pocket-book was not the case.
Perhaps Alice had grown weary of London life
and they had returned to Seafern; or they might
be again travelling on the Continent. His sur-

prise gave place to a feeling of disappointment at
this unlooked-for delay. His journey seemed
likely to be a fruitless one; but seeing the street
door open he entered the house, thinking he might
possibly meet some one there who could tell him
whither the late tenants had gone.

It was with a strange sense of mingled pain and
pleasure that he passed through the deserted
rooms, picturing how they had once been conse-
crated by the presence of Alice. "If these walls
could speak," he thought, "what might they not
tell me of the thousand ways in which she made
home beautiful? It is almost impossible to believe
that these dull rooms ever echoed her laughter,
her light step, and her sweet voice, for they are
dreary enough now."

On the first floor he met a man who appeared to
be the landlord, for he greeted Sydney with the
summary of the house's advantages and the good
fortune it would be for any gentleman of substantial means to become his tenant. He looked crest-
fallen when Sydney replied—

"Doubtless you are right; but I am not in
search of a house at all. My only reason for

troubling you is that I thought you might be able to tell me something about my friend Mr. Fenwood."

The landlord was not a man possessing striking delicacy of feeling; he had been a bricklayer once, and was apt to remark that he had "climbed the ladder of life by caring for nobody, and he wasn't going to begin to do so now." Still, he was not unkindly, and a shadow of genuine concern passed across his face as he said in a lower voice —

"Were you a friend of Mr. Fenwood's, sir ? I'm sorry for that."

"Sorry—why ?"

"I can't wrap things up in fine words, sir; and I may as well tell you the truth at once—Mr. Fenwood is dead."

Sydney tried to realize the full meaning of these words, but could not.

"Dead !" he repeated faintly.

"Ay, sir. I didn't think you'd ha' taken it so much to heart, or I might have told you in a more roundabout way; but I always was a blunt man, and there's no use denying it. You look pale and ill, sir—let me get you a little brandy."

"No, thank you," replied Sydney, making a strong effort to collect his thoughts; "I will rest here a few minutes if you will allow me, and then I shall require no other medicine but the fresh air. Your words bewildered me—I can hardly believe them now; we had known each other from boyhood. Dead—is it possible, and he so young?"

The last words were spoken to himself rather than addressed to the landlord, who watched him silently as he stood with his elbow resting on the mantelpiece and his eyes fixed dreamily on the uncarpeted floor. Never until that moment had he known how dear his old schoolfellow was to him, and all the feelings of anger and resentment he had recently cherished came crowding round him like reproachful shadows; but he had learnt the difficult lesson of self-control too well for its strength long to desert him now, and when he spoke again the landlord was surprised at the recovered firmness of his voice.

"I am stronger now, and need not trouble you any longer. Is there a cab-stand near here?"

"It's some little distance, sir; but if you'll allow me, I'll fetch you a cab."

"You are very kind—I am ashamed to trouble you, but"—

Without giving him time to finish the sentence, the man hurried into the street, leaving Sydney alone in the deserted house. In that moment he did not think calmly of anything: all was confused and nothing certain, except the sense of pain. When the cab arrived, he thanked the landlord mechanically, gave the driver the name of the nearest hotel he knew, and was only vaguely conscious of passing in some way—he could hardly tell how—through the crowded streets until they reached their destination. He had stayed here before, and was greeted by one of the waiters with respectful recognition. In the same abstracted mood he paid the cabman what he asked without clearly understanding what it was, and requested to be shown into a private room.

But when the waiter had officiously given the apartment a few altogether unnecessary arranging touches—as has been the custom of his class from time immemorial—when he had with more practical utility stirred the drowsy fire till it sprang into a cheerful blaze—when he had received a negative reply to his inquiry whether there was

anything else he could do, and had retired shutting
the door behind him—when in short Sydney felt
that he was alone, and beyond the danger of his
reflections being interrupted, he began to think
more collectedly of what he had that morning
heard.

In every reverie, however tangled and contradictory, there is generally one dominant feeling
which shapes and colours all the rest. In the
present case this emotion was one of tender remembrance, as he recalled all the scenes of their
intimacy—trivial and long-forgotten incidents
returning as freshly to his mind as if they were
being re-enacted before his eyes. It has been
already said that his love for his old schoolfellow
had in it something romantic and chivalrous, as
the affection of a strong nature for a weak one,
which it benefits and protects with large-hearted
gentleness, always has.

The events of school life had bound them closely
together, and it was of this period he thought
most—of exploits in the class-room and the cricket
field—between the goals at football and in the
rowing boats on the river. Unimportant conver-

sations repeated themselves—he remembered with strange clearness a paper chase when he and Percy had been the hares; and his younger companion had declared himself exhausted just when they were within thirty feet of home, and half a dozen of the hounds were in full pursuit fifty yards behind. It seemed only yesterday since that moment when he had taken the little fellow in his arms, and won the game by fairly carrying him to the place of refuge. In the same way he thought of lessons where Percy failed or distinguished himself, and then with new bitterness came the heavy consciousness that the young life was over, and the chain of their friendship roughly snapped in two.

He had asked for no particulars concerning Percy's death—partly from his sense of inability to sustain any conversation, and partly from an instinctive perception that information on this head must be gained in another quarter. Musing on the people who would be most likely to give it to him, he thought of Mr. Greville, whom he knew slightly, and who was more likely to have been in Percy's confidence than any one.

Sydney determined to call on him the next day, and to postpone all plans for his own future until after the interview. The waiter observed with some surprise that he sent away his dinner untouched—was grave and silent, and retired early to bed.

"I never did believe in furrin parts," he remarked in confidential conversation with the cook. "Mr. Mayfield used to be as bold a gentleman as ever added a handsome gratuity to his bill; since he has been among the Maunseers, and the Prooshans, and the cannibals, and sich-like" (the waiter's geographical ideas and his conceptions of the customs of other races were somewhat hazy) "he seems crushed like, and ain't the same man. Well for my part, I say, give me London, and thank 'eavin I was born a Englishman."

CHAPTER XIII.

What find I here,
Fair Portia's counterfeit ? What demi-god
Hath come so near creation ? Move these eyes ?
Or whether, riding on the balls of mine,
Seem they in motion ? Here are sever'd lips,
Parted with sugar breath ; so sweet a bar
Should sunder such sweet friends. Here in her hairs
The painter plays the spider ; and hath woven
A golden mesh to entrap the hearts of men,
Faster than gnats in cobwebs. But her eyes—
How could he see to do them ? having made one,
Methinks, it should have power to steal both his,
And leave itself unfurnish'd : yet look, how far
The substance of my praise doth wrong this shadow
In underprizing it, so far this shadow
Doth limp behind the substance.
                              MERCHANT OF VENICE.

NEXT morning Sydney called at the office of Messrs.
Greville and Wynch, and inquired for the senior
partner. One of the clerks informed him that Mr.
Greville was at that moment engaged with a client
in a private room, but that he would probably be
at liberty in a few minutes. The lawyer's conversation seemed to have an effect the reverse of
soothing upon his companion, who frequently
raised his voice to a pitch that caused his words

to pass in spectral fashion through the closed door; and occasionally to become audible to the listening clerks beyond, who appeared to find the monotony of legal affairs greatly relieved by this incident.

At length the indignant client who had been so loudly chafing at the law's delays appeared in the outer office, his verbal exertions and his sense of wrong making him emerge from the conference in a heated and flushed condition, which caused him to repeatedly pass a coloured silk handkerchief across his brow, muttering angrily all the while. As soon as the combustible litigant had gone, Sydney sent in his card requesting the favour of a few minutes' conversation : the clerk promptly returned with a message to the effect that Mr. Greville was now disengaged and would see him immediately.

" This is an unexpected pleasure Mr. Mayfield," said the lawyer, motioning him to a chair, and nodding the clerk an intimation to close the door and leave them. " I thought you were hundreds of miles away."

" I measured the distance by thousands a fort-night ago, for I only arrived in Liverpool yesterday morning: Mr. Greville, I know your time is valuable, and I will not waste it by a tedious introduction to what I have to say. You know that Percy Fenwood and I were friends from boyhood."

"I had forgotten, but I remember now that you remind me of the fact—yes —yes, a sad story that."

"Until yesterday," pursued Sydney, "I believed him to be living, and I was unspeakably shocked and pained by being abruptly informed of his death. I have come here because (although professional confidence is sacred), I thought as you were his friend as well as his legal adviser, you might be able to tell me the cause of his death and the circumstances that succeeded it."

Mr. Greville hesitated, and seemed for two or three minutes in doubt whether he should speak freely or not; but at last he said—

"You could have no interested motives for your inquiries Mr. Mayfield—at all events not what the law calls interested; and besides these things are not known to me professionally merely—I daresay half a dozen people know them too—I will speak, so far as I am at liberty to do so, and rely upon your honour to respect my confidence."

With this introduction Mr. Greville gave Sydney a hasty outline of Percy's life during the last two years. It was necessarily brief and imperfect, but Sydney already held the clue in his hands, and with the assistance of the lawyer's scattered hints and statements, appreciated the truth only too well. Although the narrative occasioned him deep pain he listened calmly, and without betraying any surprise, until its conclusion, when he said quickly—

"Ruined—everything sold—nothing whatever saved from the fire—it seems impossible."

" It is true nevertheless I assure you. The poor boy would have wasted a fortune five times as large if he had had the chance. He speculated recklessly and I doubt if Fortunatus's purse would have been enough for him."

"And Mrs. Fenwood?" (Sydney had not mentioned her name until he could trust himself to do so, and now uttered it with apparently no deeper concern than friendly interest.) "Do you know what has become of her?"

"I'm sorry to say I do not. She had an illness after her husband's death; and I had to act a great deal on my own responsibility, but when she recovered she told me she should look for an engagement as governess, or companion—since then I have not seen her."

"You did not think it necessary then to offer her any assistance," said Sydney unable to repress a feeling of rising scorn; "I should have thought that remembering your long friendship with the family at Seafern Hall, you might have shown a little more consideration."

Mr. Greville had been quite unmoved during the declamatory denunciation of his client with the brazen lungs; but he winced and coloured slightly at these last words.

"You do me an injustice," he said, "indeed you do; I lost sight of Mrs. Fenwood during my absence in Paris. I sent her my address there, and asked her to write if I could help her in any way; but if she sent a letter I never received it. I told her she might draw on me if she needed money, but she has not done so, and I have been unable to learn anything of her whereabouts."

Seeing that nothing more was to be learnt from Mr. Greville, Sydney apologised for having detained him so long, and left the office. His calm face was a striking contrast to the perspiring physiognomy of the excited client; yet it may be questioned whether that victim of tape, parchment, and legal quibbles, had such deep cause for mental disquietude. It almost maddened him to think Alice might at that moment be feeling the hitherto unknown bitterness of poverty, in the patient fulfilment of uncongenial drudgery, or the constrained endurance of insults from vulgar wealth, or high-born frivolity. He longed to find her out—to lay all he possessed at her feet, and win one more glance from the unforgotten beauty of her eyes; but it was folly he felt, to indulge in such wild dreams; and there would be absolute baseness in the idea of intruding upon her in her grief, and using her poverty or her helplessness as a pretext for thrusting his love upon her. Still the thought of her being alone and friendless was unbearable to him—he must find out where she was, and be guided by the nature of his discovery. The circumstances of her life must be exceptional indeed, if they precluded the possibility of his serving her in any way—of his contributing in some small degree to her happiness,

without her knowing from whence this consideration came. His plans were of necessity vague, but
they did not seem to him impracticable; and he
felt an impatient longing to reduce them to
accomplished facts. In all this his primary motive
was not a selfish one; the thought that perhaps a
far-off day might come when his unwavering constancy might be rewarded by her undivided love,
may have been a silent factor in his reflections, for
passion may be pure and noble, but was probably
never quite disinterested; still his first and leading thought was to benefit her; and for that end
he would not only have made the easy, because
brief, sacrifice of life, but the harder sacrifice of
all that makes life worth having.

After some reflection, he decided to go to Seafern, and endeavour to glean some particulars
there; but the restless spirit of change had in-
vaded even this quiet sanctuary, and he saw
everywhere that greater alterations might be
looked for in the future. There was much talk of
bringing the railway to the sleepy little village,
and some steps had already been taken towards
that once undreamt-of consummation. What

further changes should he find? Mr. Greville had
told him that Seafern Hall was sold—should he
find the church pulled down, and a new one in
course of erection? He was quite relieved by
his first glimpse of its familiar ugliness, and rang
the vicarage bell with a pleased anticipation of
the coming interview. A strange servant opened
the door, and answering his question whether the
vicar was in, in the affirmative, ushered him into
the library, saying her master would be down
directly.

Sydney looked round the room with some surprise—the furniture seemed unfamiliar, and
brighter than of yore—the shelves contained a
number of valuable works, suggesting profounder
erudition than Mr. Ellis had ever possessed, and
while he was wondering at the transformation, he
distinctly overheard the voices of children playing
in the room above. What could all this mean?
Was he to be menaced with another disappointment? At this moment the door opened, and a
clergyman entered the room, but not the one
whom Sydney was expecting. Instead of the
athletic form, piercing eyes, and crisp curling grey

hair of Mr. Ellis, he saw a young man of slight figure, pale studious face, and faultless dress, who wore spectacles, and seemed to find considerable difficulty in immediately concentrating his attention upon his visitor, partly from constitutional absent-mindedness, and partly from an uneasy sense that the noise upstairs was increasing.

"Is there anything I can do for you sir?" he said, in a pleasing though rather weak voice. "I do not think I have had the pleasure of meeting you before."

"I have been absent from England for some time," said Sydney, "and called to see Mr. Ellis, the former vicar in this place. Is his absence temporary, or has he left altogether?"

Mr. Rickley (that was the young clergyman's name) looked pained and surprised; for a few moments he was silent—then with great delicacy and manly feeling he told the story of the lifeboat and the burning ship, dwelling on the brave man's heroism, and the power which that evening's unselfish courage had upon the hearts of the villagers.

The tears started to Sydney's eyes as he lis-

tened—not of pity, but of pride and joy. He
almost envied the simple-hearted clergyman a
death, a rest, and a memory, like this; for the
world never seems drearier, than when we hear
that some brave heart has left it.

"Was he an intimate friend of yours?" inquired Mr. Rickley.

"I had not that honour, for believe me I should
have esteemed it one. My acquaintance with him
was very slight, but long enough for me to respect
and admire him. I am indebted to you for your
courtesy and consideration; but I will not tres-
pass on your indulgence any longer."

"Our unfashionable mid-day dinner will be
ready in a few minutes—can I prevail upon you to
stay? If you know anything of the village we
shall not have difficulty in finding subjects of
mutual interest, even apart from the great world
that lies beyond it."

At any other time Sydney would probably have
accepted this invitation; but he had further inquiries to make in the village, and wished to return
to London the same day; moreover he happened
to glance from the vicar to his wife, a pale slight

girl about four-and-twenty, who had entered the
room a minute or two before; and fancied he read
in her face a pathetic consciousness that her house-
keeping arrangements were on too limited a scale
for the entertainment of unexpected guests. This
decided him, and expressing a hope that an acquaintance so sadly commenced might be continued under brighter auspices, he left them.

Sauntering among the fishermen's cottages, he
felt the existence of the Seafern known in old
days more strongly than he had done yet. Here
there was little change—babies had become
children, and children had grown into stout lads
and pretty lasses. A few familiar faces were gone,
and he occasionally met strangers who had taken
their places; but the general aspect of things was
unaltered. He had two or three hours to spare,
and spent the time in strolling about the village
and talking to old fishermen whom he had once
known, and with whom he had been a general
favourite.

He had thought of visiting Sunrise Peak, or
some other of their favourite walks: but his
courage failed him—the evening when he and

Alice had watched the sunset together, before their first parting, had something of bitterness in its remembrance; and to stand upon the same spot, knowing she was desolate, sorrowful, and far away, would be more than he could bear. He had intended also to have one last glimpse of Seafern Hall; but they told him the old building was being pulled down, and he could no more have watched calmly the destruction of what was associated in his heart with memories tender and sacred, than he could have watched a living thing torn limb from limb. The savage instinct which prompts men to destroy rarely extends to delight in witnessing destruction; and when we see anything we have loved—inanimate and senseless though it may be—reduced to a chaotic heap of useless fragments, it seems as if our life had been pulled down, and its most cherished ideals scattered ruthlessly to the winds.

Among other things Sydney learnt at Seafern was the story of Miss Gordon's marriage and departure to Glasgow. One of the girls who had been in her class at the Sunday-school, and still wrote to her occasionally, gave him the address, which in lieu of any better discovery he was grateful to have.

"I may get the clue I want here," he thought, when he was once more on his way to London. "I don't fancy Miss Gordon was ever particularly fond of me, and I daresay she doesn't forget her dismal experience of the sea, when she thought it her duty to be Alice's chaperon; but perhaps marriage has softened her—at any rate she can't do me any harm, and it's possible she may tell me what I want to know."

So two days later he made his appearance at Mrs. McTurgot's house, much to that lady's astonishment, who had as little expected a visit from the Emperor of China. The wedded life of this exemplary matron was more tranquil and contented than many an existence which has been marked by a bright and romantic wooing. She told Sydney she was happy—Mr. McTurgot was very kind to her; and although she admitted with judicial impartiality that he had his faults, she appeared to think on the whole he was not worse than other men—in many respects she considered he was better; for he did not break any of the

Ten Commandments, and took only one glass of whiskey and water after supper, whereas his friend Mr. McCronshaw (who was five years older, and also an elder) was never satisfied with less than three.

On the whole Sydney considered his old acquaintance improved, and silently wondered what the cause could be, not readily attributing this augmented wealth of soul or mind to the somewhat tame virtues of Mr. McTurgot. But after he had been a little while in the house she brought him her baby, a child of twelve months old; and he no longer wondered that she possessed greater animation, and consequently greater interest than of old. Judged by a purely impartial standard, this scion of the house of McTurgot could scarcely be pronounced beautiful. He had his mother's clear blue eyes, it is true, but the paternal nose which the son faithfully inherited, was the reverse of Grecian—the complexion had already become doubtful, and the cheek bones gave promise of being higher than is quite in accordance with southern taste.

But his mother bent over him with tenderness

and pride; and as Sydney watched how the sight
of the little one could brighten her eyes, and bring
a rosy light to her face, for the first time in his
life he almost admired her.   After all, she was not
without womanly feeling, though her disposition
was to hide every trace of it from sight; and her
views of life taught her to regard all that was
strongest and best in her character as weak and
foolish.

Of Alice she could tell him nothing, and said
with tears in her eyes, which seemed so alien to
that serene region, that they quitted it as soon as
possible —

"I only knew a week ago of Percy's death.   I
call him Percy Mr. Mayfield, for I knew him when
he was a child, and loved him always though he
was so troublesome.   I wondered why Alice didn't
write to me, for until the last few months she
always did so; but I understand now.   She knows
the many causes I have for being grateful to her,
and how glad I should be to show it, now that she
is poor and wanting friends.   But she is proud —
she always was; and she considers Mr. McTurgot
a little too—a little too prudent; and so she pre-

fers that I should think she has forgotten me, to putting it in my power to offer her a home."

So here again the information Sydney wanted was not to be found: he accepted however a pressing invitation to stay to dinner, in which Mr. McTurgot himself (who shortly after made his appearance) cordially joined. Sydney was rather curious to observe the character of hospitality practised in this home; but somewhat to his surprise he found it to be strikingly generous—the merchant belonging to that numerous class to whom hospitality is an instinct, although parting with money is like renouncing love, hope, and fair fame.

On his return to London, his inquiries were not more successful. In vain he endured long conversations with all of Alice's acquaintances whom he knew, contriving to introduce some casual reference to his old friend into the discussion, but always with the same result. They remembered Alice very well—they had been to parties at her house, during the first season after her marriage; but for some time they had not met, and since her husband's death they had lost sight of her altogether. Equally fruitless were his inquiries at governess agencies—his constant scrutiny of the advertisement column of the *Times,* and his frequent attendance at churches, where he thought there was any probability of finding her: three months passed in this search without a clue, and he began to think he was pursuing a shadow, and perhaps she had left the country altogether.

One morning as he was walking disconsolately along, he met Mr. Halliday, the architect in whose office he had formerly held a confidential position, and who greeted him now with undiminished cordiality.

"Why Sydney my boy," said the old man heartily, "I thought you were at the Antipodes."

"I have not been in England very long, Mr. Halliday."

"I hope not, or you would have no excuse for not coming to see me. What are you doing this evening?"

"Nothing particular."

"Then I shall expect you to dinner. You remember the address, and the hour—half-past six punctually, and I wouldn't have the soup spoilt by putting it back for the Three Estates of the realm, to say nothing of that democratic rabble which calls itself the Fourth;" and without waiting for a reply, the architect hurried from him, recognising another acquaintance in the distance.

They were quite alone that evening, with the exception of Mr. Halliday's niece—a pale timid girl, whose speech consisted entirely of monosyllables; and who seemed to experience considerable difficulty in uttering these. There is contagion in a companion of this sort. Mr. Halliday's conversational powers were not remarkable, and Sydney's experiences since his arrival in England had not tended to raise his spirits. On the whole, therefore, although from a material point of view, the dinner left nothing to be desired—as a meeting of " God-created souls," it was open to the charge of failure. When the silent maiden retired from the room, however, Mr. Halliday said suddenly—

" Sydney, my boy, there's something on your mind. I don't ask what it is; but I see one thing very clearly—idleness is not to your taste, and the sooner you get into harness again the better."

Sydney coloured, for the first words touched

a secret wound, and the practical advice only echoed a conviction which daily presented more definite shape to his own thoughts.

" I never intended to go through life without a profession," he said, " I don't think I should do so if my income were twenty times as great as it is. I hold that a definite aim is a necessity for every man ; but somehow I seem to have lost mine."

Mr. Halliday caught at the last words—

" Come back to us," he said, " the only foolish thing I ever knew you do, was to change your mind about those articles of partnership, when nothing was wanting to make them binding but your signature. The fellow who tried to take your place is leaving me. He is an ass, and hasn't brains enough to be the architect of a coal-scuttle. You and I always got on well together— I'm getting old now—I'm richer than I ever was, and I don't see why I should be worried with every miserable trifle that goes beyond the narrow compass of that dolt's ability. Come—I see you waver, and with you to hesitate in a refusal, is a certain indication that you mean to consent."

" You don't know whether my wanderings have

made me as incorrigible as the gentleman you criticise so sharply," said Sydney with a smile.

"I'll take my chance of that—you know my old way of liking a definite answer. Which is it to be—yes or no?"

"I appreciate your kindness fully Mr. Halliday. It would be a poor return if I accepted your offer, and then in a month or two became restless, and abruptly resigned the position you so generously offer. Still you know the direction in which my sympathies and ambition used to point; and if I can take up the old threads, believe me I will gladly do so. Let us arrange it this way—I will come to your office and see how far my heart and energy can give their strength to the old pursuits —let the rest be three months; at the end of that time we shall see our respective positions more clearly. Until then I cannot accept any salary; but I ask instead, the sense of perfect freedom."

Mr. Halliday regarded this compromise, as not altogether satisfactory: but was too glad to renew his connection with Sydney on any terms to oppose it. The experiment was successful—after a few days it seemed to Sydney as if the chain of his duties had scarcely been broken at all; and at the end of the three months, the agreement of partnership was drawn up once more, and this time duly signed and witnessed, with all needful formality.

To Mr. Halliday and others, Sydney seemed quite unaltered—he gave to his work the old strength of perception, energy, and will. Travel and time seemed to have increased his ability; and it was easy to perceive that no other profession would have been so congenial to him; but to himself, half the charm of occupation was gone— he no longer felt ambitious, and listened almost with listless indifference, when his suggestions or designs were approved or praised.

One morning he was walking through Gracechurch Street, and wondering if he should ever recover his old elasticity of temperament; when his eyes fell upon a face that made the hot blood flush to his cheek, and his heart beat faster, while his lips involuntarily uttered the word—

"Alice."

It was a momentary illusion—in another instant he realized the truth. He was standing by a picture-dealer's window, where the most prominent object was a life-size portrait of the woman he loved. The stream of pedestrians flowed rapidly past him, each so intent on his own interest, as to have little leisure for observation; now and then some idler stopped to gaze for a minute at the pictures displayed in the window; but even these passed on without noticing how he stood fascinated by beauty, and unable to move.

The portrait he was contemplating had no romantic interest apart from his own associations: it had been painted by an English artist, whom Percy had met at Rome on his wedding tour. At that time he was prouder of his fair young wife than of anything else in the world; and had insisted in spite of Alice's protestations, that she should give the painter an opportunity of proving his skill. The work commenced at Rome, had been completed in London; and although not in the highest style of art, was no mean indication of the artist's power.

To Sydney the painting seemed vivid with glowing life—he had never seen her so richly dressed before; but the easy grace of her attitude—the perfect proportions of her tall queenly figure—the heavy tresses of her luxuriant hair—the proud light of her deep brown eyes—the statuesque refinement of her features, and the rosy sweetness of her mouth, had haunted his waking and sleeping dreams for years.

How long he stood feasting his eyes on the picture, which had so often presented itself to his unaided imagination, he never knew; but at last he realized that this spell was wrought not by a great magician, but by a few feet of canvas, which something less than the wealth of Aladdin would be sufficient to purchase.

With this thought he entered the shop, and indicating the portrait by a gesture, abruptly asked the dealer his price. The man looked at him with some curiosity—he had bought the picture himself at the general sale of Percy's effects, at a price so low, as to make loss on the purchase almost impossible. Portraits were not easily disposed of he knew; but the face here represented was so fair, that it occurred to him it would be an attractive feature in his window, even if nobody were disposed to buy it.

Sydney's impulsiveness betrayed his knowledge of the original, and the dealer doubled his price accordingly. Even this amount however was not large, and Sydney wrote the needful cheque without a moment's hesitation, giving the direction where it was to be sent, with a sense of triumph which he strove unsuccessfully to suppress, wondering the while that so great a prize could be obtained by so slight an effort.

And so in the apartments he had taken, there hung one picture from which he derived more delight and companionship than the wealthiest connoisseur ever gained from galleries of art. To study its exquisite beauty of form and tint was not without pain—there were times when its presence had in it an element of mockery, reminding him that this shadow was all the reward he had gained for his years of constant worship and passionate devotion. But love's pain is better than any other pleasure; and in course of time he came to regard the picture with a kind of pagan reverence—to fancy he read in its smile, approval or sympathy; and to consider its beauty a divine influence surrounding him, robbing his loneliness of the sense of solitude; and making his cheerless lodging-house a home.

CHAPTER XIV.

"What matter with what words I woo'd her? She said I had
   misunderstood her.
  Misunderstood! misunderstood! . . . . Ay, not her only, but
   thereby
  All that souls say in flesh and blood! misunderstanding till I
   die
  The meaning of that face, the while my heart lay aching in its
   smile."

OWEN MEREDITH.

MUCH has been written and more said of the subtle
sympathy existing between twin souls — of the
intuitive perception which reads the unspoken
language of thought—which instinctively foresees
coming triumph or impending grief; and that
such sympathies do exist, notwithstanding the
sceptical sneers with which belief in them has
been assailed, would be readily asserted by a crowd
of witnesses under five-and-twenty, whose young
hearts beat to the sweet rhythm of the old, old
song—

> " C'est l'amour—l'amour—l'amour—
> Qui fait le monde à la ronde."

But be the truth of this as it may, the negative statement of the same proposition will scarcely be denied. Thoroughly discordant natures soon recognise each other; and if they are compelled by force of circumstances to live together, it is remarkable what ingenious multiplicity of variations will be found to the old airs of torture and irritation. The subject of mothers-in-law—those benignant fairies of a home, who diffuse a soft lustre on the affairs of everyday life—is too important a theme for parenthetical discussion; but when an allusion is made to the enforced companionship of uncongenial spirits, with what unseemly haste do the images of husbands, wives, uncles, and cousins, come crowding on our minds.

Alice's first experience of life in the Staffords' house was not encouraging. Neither her uncle nor his wife were distinctly unkindly in spirit, or harsh in manner; but the school of prudential interest, is not favourable to the development of any emotions, not comprised in the somewhat narrow limits of the multiplication table. It is surprising how many objects can be squeezed into·

the compass of the smallest mind; and among this miscellaneous furniture, it is noticeable that every one has a miniature pantheon of his own—where the secret incense is burnt with more earnestness and the prayers uttered with more depth of feeling than is observable in the larger temples, dedicated to the worship of the one acknowledged God.

Both Mrs. Stafford and her husband acted in accordance with the general rule; and a prominent niche in their sanctuaries, was given to the idol of success. Let them not be blamed for this, the golden deity has many worshippers; and probably a day never passes, without the fragrant sacrifice of well-cooked dinners, and the costly libation of rare wines, being offered before his shrine.

But from a practical point of view (and who is foolish enough to take any other?) Alice was not successful. A young widow, with no wealth but rare beauty and a brave heart, is an object for compassion doubtless; but scarcely for sympathy or affection, especially if disaster has been caused by ignorance of the world's ways; and an inability to wrestle with it. Mrs. Stafford would have been

sincerely glad of any good fortune coming to her
niece, provided it was in no way detrimental to
herself; but she did not at all regard it as a necessity
to offer her so intangible a commodity as gentleness or love.

Alice felt the altered atmosphere of her new
home so deeply, that had it not been for the younger
children, she would probably not have stayed there
a week. At this time Walter was away—travelling for his father in the North; and Mr. Stafford,
though kinder than his wife, frequently did not
return home till late at night; and then was often
so preoccupied with business affairs, as to give little
or no attention to the circle immediately around
him. This gave Mrs. Stafford undisputed possession of the field, and she found the task of
reading Alice frequent homilies on the sins of
extravagance, and the deadly vice of poverty, an
occupation at once virtuous and agreeable.

And Ethel?

She had called herself Alice's friend—she had
written her letters abounding in expressions of
enthusiastic attachment—she had lavished caresses
upon her, and declared the world contained nothing

for which she cared so much. Although she had but a faint remembrance, she could not so utterly obliterate all this from her memory, as to be able to avow open hostilities. Still she took no pains to conceal that a change had swept across the horizon—that the poor cousin must not expect the consideration she had received when she was rich —that a girl who was half a dependent in her father's house, must not be surprised at being made the victim of caprice. Perhaps Ethel could not repress a sense of jealousy—there was no doubt in her own mind touching the superiority of her own style of beauty to Alice's; but men were often foolish, and might possibly arrive at a different conclusion; especially as she saw with secret dissatisfaction that now Alice's boating experiences were two years in the background, the hands whose sunburnt hue she had triumphantly observed, were now as soft and white as her own.

But Alice's pupils, Nellie and Daisy, loved her as something prettier and kinder than they had ever known before. It happened about this time that Daisy, the baby as they called her, betrayed feverish symptoms, and seemed on the eve of a

serious illness. The alarm proved groundless—it
was only a childish disorder; but while it lasted
the little sufferer would have no nurse but Alice.
No one else seemed so strong and gentle—no one
else could lift her so tenderly—could give her food
or drink with so caressing a hand—could beguile
the heavy hours by song or story with such sweet
success. Mrs. Stafford saw all this, and the spectacles with whose assistance she was reading the
money article in the *Times* grew unaccountably
dim.

"Are you better to-day darling?" Alice asked
one morning, coming softly beside the little bed,
and laying her cool hand lightly on the flushed
forehead.

"Yes, I shall soon be well now dear Alice; but
there is one thing that troubles me."

"What is it Daisy?"

"Nellie says you are going away—that is not
true—is it?"

Alice looked lovingly on the little upturned face,
but did not answer. The home was dreary enough
to her, and she had intended to leave it; but she
had pictured her doing so without any one feeling
a regret: at the child's pleading she felt her

strength of resolution fail, and although she did not at once yield, the words—"Yes I am going," were less easy to utter than she had anticipated.

"Don't go Alice," said the child, "it will be so dull without you. Who'll nurse me if I am ill again, and who will tell me stories like you do? Ethel doesn't know them, and she won't take pains like you; but if you'll stay I'll be so good, and do all you tell me, and love you better than any one else in the world."

"Do you really want me to stay Daisy?"

The child did not answer in words, but raising herself in the bed, threw her weak little arms round Alice's neck. There was no resisting such persuasion, and when Daisy lay down to rest again her face was bright and contented; for she had received not only a caress, but the promise that she asked.

After a while Alice's life at Clapham grew more endurable. Walter's attitude to her, although rather reserved and diffident, was always chivalrous and considerate; and he did not hesitate to snub his sister if he fancied her words or actions betrayed any other conception of their cousin's position in the home than that of an equal.

Ethel too found it easier on the whole to be friendly than disagreeable. Alice could help her in so many ways; for she was naturally indolent, and the sacrifice of dignity seemed preferable to the task of darning stockings or mending gloves.

One evening she was at the piano singing, and Alice was engaged on some occupation of this kind, to their mutual satisfaction, for Ethel was never so delighted as when she could get her own work done by somebody else, while Alice always fond of music, had a special pleasure in listening to her cousin's voice. It was a mezzo-soprano of small power and compass, but sweet in tone, and highly cultivated. Ethel's fondness for poetry has been already mentioned; and if she did not actually appreciate feeling, she was no mean actress, and mimicked it well. Alice listened with a heightened colour and a thousand sweet memories crowded round her, as the words avowing the creed of love's immortality floated on the wings of a sweet melody through the room.

" The shadowy past is dead,
    You would have me think to-day;
When the sun on river and hill has shed
His glories of purple and gold and red,
    Who dreams of the moon's pale ray ?

" I'm tired of the noise and glare,
    And the mad world's sordid schemes ;
I long for the hush of the starlit air,
When love was life, and the world seemed fair
    In the haze of a thousand dreams.

" If a touch—a smile—or a tone
    Of that far-off time were lost,
The dearest wealth of my soul were gone ;
And the garden of life in an instant grown
    To a desolate waste of frost.

" The forest is strong that braves
    The storms of a thousand years—
The sea is strong with its leaping waves ;
And Death in his cold domain of graves,
    Unconquered by human tears.

" But the woodland monarchs die,
    At a Dryad's mournful call—
The ocean's stream shall at length be dry—
The stars shall fail in the summer sky,
    And the dreaded sceptre fall ;
But the heart that loves has a deeper strength,
    And a life beyond them all."

As if the song had been a spell to conjure up the absent and forgotten, the last words had scarcely died away when a servant entered the room with a card that she handed to Ethel, who read aloud in no very amiable or gratified tone the name— "*Mr. John Heatherly.*"

"Did you say I was at home?" she inquired sharply.

"Yes miss—I told him master and missis were out, and Mr. Walter was away; but he asked for you."

"I suppose I must see him—show him up."

The servant left the room, and Alice rose for the same purpose; but Ethel hurriedly interposed—

"Don't go Alice—I would much rather not be alone; and I should really like you to see him."

But Alice chose to ignore this invitation to remain: she had heard something of John Heatherly, and was determined if he wished to say anything to Ethel he should not be prevented from doing so by her presence. The drawing-room where they were sitting had two doors, one opening on to the staircase and the other leading to a smaller apartment, which was dignified by the name of the schoolroom. Alice intended to pass through this scene of her daily work, and go downstairs unnoticed; but greatly to her annoyance she found the farther door locked, and all possibility of escape cut off. She had no inclination to return to the drawing-room, and not caring to overhear the conversation there, took up a book and began to read.

At first she succeeded in abstracting her attention; but the work was a dull one, and the voices in the adjacent room grew louder. The walls were thin; and Alice soon felt it impossible not to hear the sounds which faint, yet distinct, reached her from time to time.

They spoke first of the past—the deep tones of John Heatherly's voice lingering tenderly on some evening of long ago; and Ethel trying to banish earnestness by light words and musical laughter.

Then not without diffidence and hesitation, Walter's former tutor spoke of the present and the future. He told her of an appointment he had recently gained as librarian to a college, which although not brilliant was definite and promised well. He spoke of the further prospects it opened—of the congenial nature of the occupation—of the increased facility it would give him for deeper study; and then his hesitation gave place to rapid fluency as he spoke of her.

He said the thought of her had been with him in all his struggles, inspiring him with a power greater than his own poor abilities—he told her how he had loved her from the first moment they had met, but had not dared to hope she would ever deign to care for him till she had herself assured him of the fact—he spoke of himself with modesty —of his love with confidence and pride. He was only a poor scholar, whose whole life had been spent among books, and who knew little of the world and its ways; but there was something great in the strength of the love he gave her, at once devoted and unselfish—passionate and pure.

At last there came a pause, while he waited for Ethel's answer. That young lady had never even imagined emotions so deep as these, and felt rather disconcerted and frightened by their utterance; but at length she controlled her voice, and recovering her self-possession, answered in a way which would have delighted the soul of her mother beyond all measure.

She dismissed the past with a brief allusion— they had been very young, at least she had; and of course it would be absurd to attach any importance to the foolish words spoken long ago— she was very glad to hear of Mr. Heatherly's success, and hoped the fairest fortune lay before him in the future—she should always esteem him as a friend, and be grateful to him for his kindness to her brother (there was a faint touch of intentional coarseness in the last remark, to remind the tutor of the difference in their social positions); but as to their ever being more to each other than friends, that was impossible. She uttered the last words in a tone so low and musical, yet so entirely without any inflection of sympathy or reluctance, that Alice almost hated her.

There was another pause—longer than the former one : at length John Heatherly said huskily—"Good-bye, Ethel—after all that has passed between us, I did not look for such words as these. But I would forgive deeper and more cruel wrongs from you ; perhaps I have been an idealist, but one cannot surrender cherished beliefs in an hour. I shall never forget Ethel Stafford, and I pray from my heart God may be gentler to her than she has been to me."

With this he left her, and when Alice re-entered the room, she found Ethel sitting alone with a very dissatisfied expression on her face. She did not regret what she had done; if the interview were repeated, she would say precisely the same things over again; but she liked to be on good terms with herself, and at that moment she found it disagreeably difficult to repress the novel sensation of self-contempt.

"I wish you had stayed in the room, Alice," said she, pettishly; "he has been saying all kinds of dreadful things, and seems quite surprised that I won't marry him on three hundred and fifty a year."

"I know all," returned Alice; "the school-room door was locked, and I was compelled to overhear everything."

Ethel pouted with pretended displeasure; but she felt secretly triumphant that Alice, who undoubtedly would be considered beautiful by many men, should realize the power of her cousin's sovereignty over hearts.

"Isn't it a pity he is so poor?" she said, in something like her usual tone. "I was really very fond of him once; but of course mamma is right, and one must not let one's feelings influence one in these matters. What do you think, Alice?"

"I will tell you; though my views may be

scarcely to your taste. To-night I hardly know which to wonder at more—that such a man as Mr. Heatherly seems should stoop to notice you, or that you should dare to slight him. I always knew your soul was shallow, and your ambition petty; but I gave you credit for some womanly feeling. It is such girls as you who make our sex contemptible in the eyes of men, so that many of them write and think about us as nothing more than pretty playthings to amuse their idlest moments."

"I don't think your position in this house justifies your talking to me like this," interrupted Ethel, with an uneasy consciousness that her burning cheeks showed she had not listened to these words unmoved.

Alice smiled rather scornfully. "You are not speaking to a lover now, Ethel," she said, "and you will not sting me by your small-souled contempt for my poverty. I have remained in this house because I love the children and they love me; but if you fancy I shall play the hypocrite to conciliate you, the mistake is yours: self-interest is not the all-powerful motive with every one that it is with you. You have slighted a true man's love—and for what? For the enjoyment of a few material comforts, and the regard or envy of people as foolish as yourself. Words are wasted upon you, I know, but it is as well we should understand each other clearly; and so I say plainly that to-night I have blushed for our relationship."

Ethel did not answer, and Alice left her, glad to escape to her own room. She felt strangely agitated, for that evening's conversation, to which she had been an unwilling listener, had stirred many unforgotten thoughts into new force. She could not forget that her own action, imperfectly understood, might seem to resemble this; for had she not married without love, and appeared to sacrifice noble feeling to selfish judgment?

"Is it possible *he* thinks of me in this way?" she mused; "if he only knew the truth, he would not do so. I did wrong, I know, but not willingly: the world was too strong for me, and I was compelled to yield. He cannot know all, but he is too good, and loved me too well once, to think me base or mean. I could not bear that bitterness, but it is not laid upon me; for I could never wrong him by a thought, and he is nobler than I."

Love has many jewels; but the loyal faith that deems doubt treachery, and is unchanged by the lonely silence of weary years, is the brightest of them all.

CHAPTER XV.

" The boy had fewer summers, but his heart
  Had far outgrown his years, and to his eye
  There was but one beloved face on earth,
  And that was shining on him."

BYRON.

ALICE expected that her frankly avowed opinion of
Ethel's attitude to John Heatherly would have
the effect of estranging them altogether, but here
she was mistaken. Ethel had not an unforgiving
nature, and found it most convenient on the
whole to ignore her cousin's uncomplimentary
candour altogether. Theologians have drawn
sharply uncompromising lines between saints and
sinners—the Church and the world ; and doubtless these decisive distinctions are very comforting
to the orthodox mind; but unfortunately like
many other human productions, they will not bear
very close examination. The sinners are incon-
sistent enough to be occasionally heroic, while the
faults and errors into which the saints are sometimes betrayed, are only too well known. In the

same way it is not always easy to classify actions under the definite headings of good and evil, the same apparent result being constantly produced by widely different causes.

Whether Ethel's reason for not cherishing resentment was due to the divine impulse of mercy, described with such grace and dignity by Portia; and finding still grander eulogy in the pages of Holy Writ; or whether it was most soothing to her self-esteem to forget accusations she had been unable to answer, it is needless to consider here. Let Sancho Panza's judgment in the case of the fatal bridge be regarded as a precedent; and the subject of inquiry have the full advantage of the doubt; she was not so rich in generous attributes that any she even seemed to possess should be willingly denied her.

One thing however is certain—her manner soon manifested the desire to conciliate Alice; and to make her think that the difference between their views was not so great after all. There is an Indian proverb to the effect that contempt even penetrates the shell of the tortoise; and the decision of Alice's words had swept her own weaker beliefs away, as the feathery crown of a dandelion is scattered by the will of the wind. Ethel was not accustomed to trouble her pretty head with questions of casuistry; and she had accepted her mother's ethics, because being the easiest and most comfortable of philosophies, it was pleasant to believe them true; but she had no depth of confidence—she was not by any means prepared to suffer for them, and consequently was impotent to battle with heart convictions, touching which she had herself a weak and sentimental sympathy.

Moreover Alice was a necessity to her—as a companion, in the shallowest sense of the word, for she understood no other—as a girl who was good-natured enough to do her work for her; and as a poor cousin who could safely be treated with insolence or caprice.

Alice read these motives clearly enough; but cared little for them, and rarely retaliated. She was beginning even to have a kind of affection for her uncle's home: he at least never thwarted her; and after a few verbal conflicts with his wife, in which that lady was decidedly worsted, she received no molestations from that quarter. It was therefore easy to tolerate Ethel, for in addition to Alice's love for the children, another interest now brightened the house.

On the rough flinty road of life, nurtured by little save the sun and rain from heaven, two wild flowers grow—love and friendship. Alice had gathered the former, and treasured it in her bosom, where it glowed and burned like fire; but the pale flower, not half so fair to look on, yet with so strangely fragrant a breath—so modest yet so enduring—so fragile yet so strong to outlive the rough touch of the tempest, and the cold scorn of time, she had never known. This gift was hers now; and the friend no other than her cousin Walter.

He was three years younger than she, and this disparity of age was not removed by any abnormal gifts of intellect or character; but he was chivalrous, generous, and enthusiastic, with quick sympathies, and high ideals. Had Alice known him under any circumstances, she would have liked the companionship of her handsome cousin; but as it was she felt so lonely and friendless—in such urgent need of escape from egotism, by affection for some one moving in a different circle of thought to herself, that it was not strange she should esteem his society the pleasantest feature of her altered life.

Love in its highest forms rarely follows the ordinary course of development; but in a single instant springs into vivid life. It is otherwise with friendship, which matures slowly, under the patient touch of time; and often the foundation of its noblest structure is simple and commonplace enough.

When Alice first came to Mr. Stafford's house, Walter said little to her, being hushed into silence by his boyish reverence for her sorrow and her beauty. But after the first two or three months, when the colour returned to her face, and a smile would occasionally play about her lips, he began to show her trifling attentions, such as bringing her home magazines and reviews, or offering her a few flowers, chosen with care that their beauty might make them acceptable, while their simplicity prevented them from assuming the character of a formal gift. From this he passed naturally enough to inducing her to read his favourite books; and at length even to their studying the same works together.

Walter's tastes had been largely formed, and indeed his whole character strongly influenced, by John Heatherly; and taking this circumstance in connection with the fact that he was scarcely nineteen, it is not strange that the authors thus selected were generally poets. Alice's education had been thoroughly practical, and the brightest and most fascinating region in the world of literature was almost unknown territory to her. This alone would have been sufficient to create a sympathy between them; and there is little cause for wonder that Walter would often look up from the book he was reading aloud, and seeing how the thoughts of a great master were reflected in her flashing eyes, would associate her in his mind with all the fairest conceptions of poetic fancy.

In this way months passed by, the summer and the autumn, which were hot and dry, being succeeded by a long and dreary winter. The season of fog and snow had been so monotonously depressing, that when the spring returned with its sweet corollaries of birds and flowers, it was as if the prison gate had been suddenly opened, and a weary term of captivity at length expired. Alice felt so at all events as actively as she had done in her childish days, when Percy had marvelled at the transformation in her moods, wrought by a passing sunbeam, or a fresh sea breeze. It was now her habit to rise early in the morning, when the rest of the household were asleep, and wander to the end of the large old-fashioned, irregular garden, which abounded in shady paths, where the luxurious companionship of leaf and blossom might be enjoyed; and thoughts of uncongenial duty and dull people be for a time completely shut out. Walter had frequently avowed his sympathy with the Sluggard of Dr. Watts' poem, and declared his belief that since Charles Lamb had exposed the fallacy of rising with the lark, it was the act of a barbarian to get out of bed before eight in the morning; but greater philosophers than he have failed to act in accordance with their theories; and after the first two or three occasions Alice had always a companion in her early morning walks.

At the end of the garden there was a rustic seat, shaded by a chestnut tree, and here they would often sit and read ; at other times they would saunter together through the winding paths in gay or earnest conversation, or if their moods were thoughtful, enjoying the loveliness of spring or early summer, in silence. Early one June morning Alice was pacing up and down their favourite walk alone, when she heard a quick step behind her, and looking round with a smile, was greeted gaily by her cousin.

" Before me as usual Alice— I thought I was early enough this morning ; but you seem to know when it is tempting out of doors instinctively, like a bird. What a glorious sky ! "

"It is very beautiful," answered Alice, looking up reverently, " the loveliness of noon seems almost coarse compared to it. It will be very hot to-day, and the close air will set me longing again for the cool plash of the waves at Seafern. Do you know the sound I mean Walter—the sound of the receding waves upon the pebbles ? That used to be music and poetry too to me when I was a child."

" Yes—I have enjoyed it many a time ; but even the air of Clapham is sweet this morning—you are surely not disposed to quarrel with it."

" No—I am on excellent terms with everything in the universe, except myself; and that is too old a discontent to be healed by sunshine. What book have you there ? "

" Shakespeare—we had just begun *The Tempest* when we were interrupted. I don't mean to do all the work however, so I have brought two copies, and you shall take your part."

He drew a small volume from his pocket as he spoke, and handed it to her. She glanced over it, with a look of pleased anticipation, as she said—

" I am selfish and prefer listening, but you have so often given me my own way that I must yield for once."

" If I were unscrupulous I should study my own inclination and leave the whole play in your hands ; but I'll be forbearing, and only give you the part of ' Miranda.' Fail to read every word of hers, however, at your peril."

Walter had a musical voice, and read well at any time ; but this morning it seemed to Alice

that his acting—if acting, indeed it was, and not
the utterance of genuine feeling—had an unusual
power. When they reached the first scene of the
third act her attention was concentrated on the book
to sustain her own part, or she must have noticed
how his voice deepened into tones of passion.

At its conclusion he said abruptly—

" You are like ' Miranda.' "

" I'm only like her in ignorance of the world,
and in having lived an uneventful lonely life
beside the sea. How exquisite that last scene is,
and I never heard you read so well. The whole
thing seems so real to me that I can't help fancying 'Prospero's' cell must have been like a favourite
cave of mine at Seafern. That shows a limited
mind you will say, unable to free itself from local
prejudices; but one cannot always be wise—it is
too fatiguing."

As she spoke in a more careless tone than was
habitual to her, she laid her hand lightly on his
shoulder. To her surprise, he pressed it to his
lips and kissed it again and again.

" You foolish boy—what are you doing?" she
said wonderingly. "Is the wizard's spell not

broken yet, and do you fancy you have still a heap
of logs to carry?   You have acted your part too
well, and cannot realize that the play is over."

"Dearest Alice, I was not acting at all—you are
my Miranda; and there is nothing on earth I
would not do or suffer if thereby I could make you
love me as I love you."

The smile faded from her face, and in its place
came an expression he had never seen there
before, and whose meaning he could not read.
Surprise had its part there, but was not the
dominant feeling—that seemed rather to be one of
pain or fear as she answered—

"Dear Walter, do not wreck your own life by
cherishing a wild dream, and spare me the bitter
knowledge of even seeming to wrong you. Women
are quick to discern when they are loved, it is said,
and I believe that is true—but I never suspected
this; and if the pleasure I have felt in your society,
and not attempted to conceal, has made you fancy
otherwise, I can only beg you to forgive me.   I
thought we were friends, and the belief was
very sweet to me; but more than that we can
never be."

"I do not blame you, darling. I am wild and foolish, but not mad enough for that. I know the thought of my love is new to you—will you not give me your answer a week, a month, a year hence, and in the meantime suffer me to hope?"

She shook her head as she replied gently, but not less firmly than before—

"This is not love, Walter, but the first shadow of it. You forget I am much older than you."

"Only three years," he interrupted eagerly. "Have you no other motive?"

She did not immediately reply, but gazed dreamily across the garden: evidently for the moment she had forgotten him, and her thoughts had wandered far away; but on his repeating the question she recalled herself, and said—

"Yes—there is another motive than which there could be none stronger. Men say that women forget easily—Walter, do not believe it, for it is not true. A love scene like the one we have been reading only comes in a few lives; and in no life is it ever repeated. When you hear women have loved three or four times, you may be certain that either they are consummate actresses or else

they have not loved at all.   I have dreamed the
dream whose pain is sweeter than all other gladness: it was only a dream—yet its memory is so
powerful with me that I cannot listen to words
like yours from any man, though he were as high
above me as the stars are above this poor petty
drama which we call life."

There was silence between them for a few
moments; then Walter said—a sudden impulse
conquering his wonted hesitation on this theme—

"If you have loved with all the capacity of your
grand strong heart, there is, indeed, no hope for
me; but have you?   I have watched you narrowly,
and when you speak of your husband—which is
not often—you are gentle and tender, as you have
been to me this morning; but love like you have
been talking about means more than that.   Has
any one else cast a shadow on your life?"

Alice had been very pale during this interview;
but now the hot blood flushed her neck, and face,
and brow.   She made a hurried gesture as if to
deprecate all further questions, and said faintly—

"We have talked long enough, Walter; let us
return to the house."

" One word more—you are not angry with me for my presumption ? "

Her old manner had almost returned as she echoed incredulously—

" Angry—do you fancy me so proud as that ? I am honoured that you should care for me ; though my hasty words may not have conveyed it. We must part from this theme for ever ; but I do not do so sadly, for we are friends and cousins still— and prizes better worth winning will be within your grasp some day."

" As a proof that you forgive me, may I kiss you ? "

She smiled assent, saying—

" In token that our relationship is unchanged. You must not rob me of my friend, Walter ; I am not so rich that I can calmly spare one of the dearest of my possessions."

He kissed the sweet red lips on which the smile was playing ; and as he did so, he felt as though his boyhood had ended.

The instinct of the flesh towards health often causes the wounds of the body to heal quickly, and to leave but a faint scar as a memento of the suffering that has preceded the recovered calm; yet old wounds which are to all appearance healed have cruel pulsations of pain at times. The sorrow of the spirit is ever more subtle and enduring; and if a golden arrow rankles in the heart in the sunny spring-time when life is young it will have power to torture in the far-off future, when the trees are leafless and the frosty winds sigh mournfully across the snowy ground—when every ambition has been crushed, except the longing for the grave.

But Walter Stafford had not loved in this way: a sweet dream had swept across his boyish world changing everything into undreamt-of beauty; and to be rudely roused from such enchanted slumber is a sharp contact with reality, which means inevitably the touch of bitter pain. Still, it was only a dream, and in a little while he began rather to be grateful for the happiness of that golden reverie than to quarrel with the world for denying him its hourly fulfilment. It was vain to sigh for the possession of a woman as far removed from him as a star; but the memory of that morning's conversation was never long absent from his thoughts, and gave to their friendship a certain affection and romance which made it different to any other they might form in after years.

The walks in the early morning did not cease, and they read many a book in the shady old garden; but by tacit consent the play of *The Tempest* was never finished.

CHAPTER XVI.

"And how did the bride perform her part?
Like any bride who is cold at heart,
    Mere snow with the ice's glitter
What but a life of winter for her!
Bright but chilly, alive without stir;
So splendidly comfortless—just like a fir
    When the frost is severe and bitter."

                                        HOOD.

ACCORDING to the precedent of certain old ballads
Ethel Stafford having slighted John Heatherly's
love, and ignored the time when vows of constancy
had been uttered by her own pretty lips, ought to
have become a prey to remorse, and established
the constancy of love by drooping and dying for
the sake of the man whom she affected to disdain.

The historian's duty, however, being merely to
record facts, it must be reluctantly admitted that
except for a display of pettishness lasting a few
hours her spirits were not at all depressed. On
the contrary, she resumed the course of her life
with unaltered serenity—in other words, she
neglected everything unpleasant which was not

absolutely unavoidable, shifted responsibility on to other shoulders, and took effectual measures to enjoy herself.

She frequently succeeded, for among her childish traits were a certain careless good humour and the exaggerated appreciation of trifles. She went more into society than she had done before, and here her pretty face never failed to gain her admiration; and her raillery springing from self-complacency and high spirits rarely failed to pass for wit. In an atmosphere of homage, Ethel felt the delight which a Swiss peasant experiences in breathing mountain air; and when it was denied her she showed the longing of her soul, if not by failing health, at all events by failing temper.

The coquetry, from which perhaps, no pretty woman is absolutely free, possessed for her the grace of an art and the dignity of a science. She was a consummate mistress of a thousand little winning actions which would have been absurd in any one else, but seemed graceful and charming in her; and if it were the custom for English maidens to follow Indian usage and wear some trophy of the victims they have conquered, her slender waist might have been clasped round by a zone of such relics. It would be tedious to minutely detail her various flirtations, especially as the heroes in these episodes possessed generally only a faint shadow of individuality; but when the winter came round again, and Ethel was congratulated on attaining her twenty-second birthday, another amorous actor appeared upon the stage, who was sufficiently unlike the rest to demand special description.

He was a little man, atoning for this deficiency in stature by redundant portliness, with shrewd grey eyes, a husky voice, and a somewhat pompous manner. He was very careful in matters of dress, and always wore broadcloth of the finest description. This was perhaps an act of supererogation, as his social position could never for a moment be doubted. Wealth, like rank and genius, sometimes stamps its mark upon a man; and the stranger would indeed have been lacking in observation who failed to recognise at a glance that he was dear to the heart of his banker, and spoken of with friendship or respect by the votaries of the Stock Exchange. This truth was written in the

folds of his capacious waistcoat—in the opulent
glitter of his chain and seals—in the stiffness of
his shirt-collar—in the creaking of his boots, no
less than in the deep lines of his face and the
determined expression of his compressed, but
rather well-shaped, mouth.

His name was Bird, a circumstance which
afforded great satisfaction to his fellow-merchants.
The wit of these gentlemen was not always of the
highest and most delicate character, and their
leisure was insufficient for the production of anything like an epigram ; but here was a pun needing
only elaboration, and it is astonishing with what
ingenuity they rang changes upon it. In their
convivial moments they spoke of him as "the
Bird who laid the golden eggs," "the Bird who
had feathered his nest well," and many other
expressions of a like character. His own clerks
flippantly alluded to him as "the crow," "the
stork," "the owl," or any other feathered creature
not celebrated for beauty. The subject of all
these witticisms, however, heard few of the
rumours, and if he had would probably have been
little affected by them. It was enough for him to

know that his autograph after the words " I promise to pay " was dearly coveted ; and the name of Bird at the bottom of a cheque was likely to be far more valuable than that of Howard or Montmorency.

It must not be inferred by this brief outline that either his appearance or his character merited scorn. Except for the before-mentioned roundness of figure, and an absence of variation in his face, he was not bad-looking; and if his moral character did not soar to any heights of ideal grandeur, it was at least free from grave reproach, and could justly claim the broad cloak of comprehensive charity. In money affairs he was positive and decided, but in other matters his character had a somewhat negative nature, having attained in many ways the serene standard of respectable mediocrity.

We have the authority of the Poet Laureate for the belief that—

> " In the spring a young man's fancy
> Lightly turns to thoughts of love ;"

and it would appear that other periods of life are affected in a like manner. Mr. Bird was forty-five

—not exactly the age ascribed to Romeo; but on the other hand, he was quite young compared to many men he knew who were conventionally supposed to be worshipped by their young brides. He was rich, and a bachelor; he was fond of society, and had a vague idea that a womanly influence in his life would be a new and soothing sensation—above all, he was harassed by the reflection that if he died childless a large portion of his wealth must go to a brother whom he detested. All these considerations urged him to marry, and the period of indecision, during which he was deferred to by scheming mothers and artlessly flattered by innocent and unsuspecting maidens, abruptly ended when he saw Ethel Stafford.

She, he felt, was exactly what he wanted to complete his home—he liked a woman to be young and pretty, and she was both; it would be necessary for his wife to entertain guests of varied character, and she talked, if not wisely, at all events with an amusing fluency which was all one had a right to look for from so charming a girl. He had chosen his plate, his pictures, and his furniture with critical judgment, which had been fully justified by possession; in the same way he selected a bride, and with as little fear of the result.

His courtship was thoroughly practical and business-like, for it consisted mainly of an interview with Ethel's father, in which the lover spoke less of passion than position, and less of beauty than his banker's books. Mr. Stafford was delighted at this unlooked-for increase of the family wealth, and might possibly have expressed his feelings in an emotional tone had not a shrewd twinkle in the wooer's eyes denoted that an unaffected reply would be more acceptable. So he controlled his agitation—said he would speak to his daughter that evening, and promised to bring her answer the next day.

Ethel at first received the announcement, not with tears or blushes, but with peals of laughter. He was twice her age, she said, and was it likely she would marry a man like that when half a dozen handsome young fellows declared she was the sweetest woman in England? But her father prudently ignored this flippancy, and enlarged upon the social advantages this opportunity offered

—she would have a command of money almost unlimited, a generous and indulgent husband who would gratify all her whims and caprices, and would enjoy the admiring envy of her less fortunate friends. This was sound common-sense, and Ethel, after a little consideration, gave it her dutiful submission—a decision of which her mother (who was very devout on the subject of providential paths, and the blessings awaiting obedient daughters) cordially approved.

Mr. Stafford conveyed the state of his daughter's affections to his son-in-law elect, who received the announcement with considerable satisfaction.

"I'm too busy just now to come down," said the enraptured lover, "but say all that's proper for me to Miss Ethel. I suppose there's nothing to delay the wedding, is there? I should like it to come off at once."

"I shan't raise any obstacle," was the rejoinder; "but you had better talk it over with Ethel yourself."

When Mr. Bird arrived for this purpose two or three days later he was very graciously received, not only for the many shining qualities which made his present companionship desirable, and the prospect which the future unfolded of close and tender relationship, but because during the last few days he had sent Ethel several costly presents of jewellery; and she felt that whatever might be said for or against sonnets and serenades, the love which spoke in gold and diamonds must be a very respectable thing indeed. Thus, without a single lovers' quarrel the period of this romantic wooing ended, and the wedding day at length arrived.

"Don't you envy me, Alice?" she said gaily, as her cousin's skilful fingers arranged her long fair hair in shining braids. "You must admit that I look very pretty this morning, and my wedding dress fits exquisitely; and there never was such a day for a wedding."

Alice smiled rather sadly as she looked at her. "You are very pretty," she said; "and your hair makes me quite vain of my powers as a lady's-maid. The day is brilliant, and the dress fits in a style above all criticism; but when I begin to be envious it will need stronger temptations than these to move me."

Ethel slightly shrugged her pretty bare shoulders, and glanced from the enviable dress in question which lay upon the bed, to her little satin shoes. It was intolerable, that a cousin attired in unpretending black, should be anything else than envious.

"I know what you mean," she said pettishly, "but I don't care. I like him quite as well as any other man—except one or two perhaps; and every one says, I am acting rightly—and as for love—and dreams, and all that kind of thing, I shall see that at the opera; and can very well dispense with it in my own life."

Alice did not reply, for bitter scorn of this selfish trifling rose to her lips; and she had no wish to be a discordant element in her cousin's thoughts that day, so she helped her to put on the rich white satin dress, assisted in the arrangement of the bridal veil; and having pronounced her appearance all that could be desired, left her with a smile of pity. "She will not be unhappy," Alice thought, "at least I hope not; for he seems kind, and will give her what she cares for more than love; but I would sooner be unhappy I think, than purchase freedom from pain by the sacrifice of all that makes life worth having. Poor Ethel! so you thought I envied you—I have wealth of which you know nothing; and would not part with my few crushed flowers of memory for riches like yours multiplied a thousand times."

But this was an unaccountable heresy shared by very few friends of the bride, the general opinion was the one held by her father, that a new and most promising chapter in the family history, was that day commenced—that from this time the Staffords were people of consequence, who should not only be noticed, but deferred to.

Nothing could have been more admirable than Ethel's appearance in the church, except perhaps the faltering modesty with which she uttered her vows of heart loyalty; and the wifely contentment of her aspect as she passed down the aisle leaning on her husband's arm. The beadle declared it was beautiful, and as he had received a liberal fee that morning he must be admitted to have been a competent observer.

The same evening John Heatherly sat among his books and papers, trying in vain to concentrate his thoughts on study. His sister Agnes—a slight girl of delicate appearance, who seemed about four years younger than her brother, was sitting a few yards from him, and frequently looked from her sewing to observe the moody expression of his face. At last she laid her work down, and coming beside him said rather timidly—

" Does this pain you very much, dear ? "

He started as if her touch had rudely disturbed his reverie.

" The past becomes part of ourselves Agnes," he said, " and one cannot surrender it without a sigh. I have always thought that a temple in ruins is not so sad as to fin l the place where you have wor-shipped degraded by avaricious merchandise. See here," he added, taking a paper from the table, and putting it in her hands, " I thought I had outlived my boyish passion for rhyme ; but the language of confession becomes rhythmical by a kind of instinct ; and it is easier to tell one's secrets in masquerade, than to suffer them to walk the earth clothed in a more sombre fashion." And Agnes read from the carelessly written manuscript—

When a subtle music lingered in the flowing of the river,
  Echoed with a deeper meaning by the lark on rapid wing ;
When I watched the crocus tremble, and the new-born roses quiver,
  At the sun's hot kiss of passion and the tender touch of spring ;
Fancy led me to a garden, where the sky was cloudless ever,
  Where the nightingales and thrushes did of love and gladness
  sing.

Spring was there with bud and blossom ; but the sweet maturer
    graces
Of the summer and the autumn, in that wondrous garden lay :
Gold and purple hung the clustering fruit above the pallid faces
    Of the hyacinths and snowdrops—pale as parting lovers they ;
And a field of ripened corn was distant scarce a hundred paces ;
    Yet the bees hummed in the hedges, through the drooping
    boughs of may.

For the loveliness fantastic of that region was enchanted,
    And contrasting seasons rendered all its aspect strange and
    wild ;
There the modest primrose nestled, and the haughty tulip flaunted—
    Simple violets and daisies 'midst the grass and clover smiled ;
And a rainbow-crested fountain all the air with murmurs haunted
    Sparkling, glancing, leaping, falling like the laughter of a child.

Thus at morn ; but when the sun had sunk in crimson glory slowly,
    And the mellow moonlight softened all the earth to gentlest
    mood ;
Then I felt the scene was sacred, and the ground I stood on holy—
    Then I knelt in love and worship, moved by impulse true and
    good ;
For I felt a higher manhood strong and passionate and lowly ;
    And I knew the spot was haunted by a dream of womanhood.

*   *   *   *   *   *

Quickly came the disenchantment—soon the peace and beauty
    ended—
Soon I saw the blossoms blighted, and a canker in the fruit ;
Then a sound of ceaseless wailing with the fountain's song was
    blended,
    As the weeds and nettles grew beside the withered rose-tree's root,
Till the sky grew black with thunder—till the ruthless rain
    descended,
    And the few birds not departed, trembled terrified and mute.

All this I could think of calmly ; but my heart was wildly beating,
　When I found her bower of roses dead and withered like the rest ;
As I cried aloud—" Ah Love all other life is frail and fleeting ;
　Yet our spirits cannot alter after plighted troth confess'd."
But her face was white and changeless—still she spake no word
　　of greeting,
And her heart was hushed and silent in a cold and lifeless breast.

Agnes looked at him half in wonder—" I do not understand," she said.

"It was all a dream," he answered, "my first illusion of what she was, and what life with her might be : now she is dead to me, and I would to God I had been dead too before I learnt to hold my faith in her a folly."

"She was never worthy of such love as yours—you say truly it was a dream ; but is it over now ? Would not the perfect waking teach you to forget it ? "

He shook his head—" I shall never forget it ; but I shall rise above it some day. The knowledge that I loved—not a woman, but a shadow, would make constancy through life a visionary act of suicide, this knowledge is my strength—but ah ! little sister it is the sharpest pain of all."

CHAPTER XVII.

"Long have I sigh'd for a calm: God grant I may find it at last!"

TENNYSON.

THE indolent conjectures which Sydney Mayfield's sudden departure from England, and his two years' absence had awakened, soon died from constitutional languor. Discussion of the motives inducing the actions of their friends, is a favourite occupation with many people; but there are various proceedings which differ strangely from preconceived expectations, and so of necessity the surprise at an imprudent marriage dies away in astonishment at an incomprehensible will, which in turn gives place to wonder at the manner in which the newly enriched legatees are spending their money. Moreover Sydney had to all outward appearance resumed the former course of his life, and as Mr. Halliday's partner was rapidly gaining a position which would have atoned for more serious idiosyncrasies. His professional ability was undoubted, and his energy unvarying; perhaps his spirits were scarcely so high as they used to be, but it was natural a man should grow graver as his responsibilities increased.

It was generally supposed among his acquaintances that he must be growing miserly, as in spite of his altered position he remained a bachelor; and lived with an unpretending absence of style. But in this, as has happened once or twice before in the world's history, the self-constituted censors were mistaken; and many a poor home whose burdens he had lightened, and to whose wants he had ministered, could have testified that he was not less generous now than he had been as a boy. Had any one spoken to him of these benevolent actions, which as he kept them strictly secret, was not likely, he would have replied that they sprang from no lofty impulse of sacrifice, but from the purely selfish desire to follow pleasure. Men's views of happiness differed—some found it in fortune, in excitement—in horses, wine, or a seat in parliament; he, on the other hand, was better pleased to see wistful eyes brighten, and hollow cheeks flush with pleasure: this might be a more amiable taste than the others perhaps, but it was merely a question of disposition, and not entitled to any praise or admiration.

He believed this firmly, and was not altogether wrong, although a character whose selfishness takes the form of ministry to others, has little in common with the popular and prevalent spirit of money-getting, which is at heart the apotheosis of sensual greed. The same impulse which had prompted Sydney to escape the pettiness of personal feeling by seeking companionship with the serene or impassioned loveliness of nature, now induced him to widen his sympathies in some self-forgetting way, while living in London. For whenever he suffered his thoughts to rest upon the course of his own life, the remembrance that the highest hope of his heart had been thwarted, and the dearest ambition of his mind had been crushed, pursued him with the persistency of a shadow.

In course of time he came to regard her portrait with a reverence almost superstitious; as an old musician feels for the violin, which has whispered his dearest secrets to his fancy, until it seems to gain the living individuality of a friend; and be--

comes a thing to be loved and feared. Imagination is the mother of all art; and it is not strange that watching the pictured face so often, he should invest it with a thousand contrasting feelings: now it seemed to him to express love or compassion—now forgetfulness or scorn: at one time it represented the girl who had rowed with him past the fishermen's cottages—at another a proud lady who had no remembrance of the past. But through all these fancies, shadowy, changing, and contradictory as they were, one constant idea remained; and stung him with a sense of impotence—the thought of her unhappiness, and when he sprang from his chair by the fireside, shook these morbid musings off, and gazed calmly at the painting on the wall, he was confronted by lips that seemed to tremble while they smiled, and eyes in whose sweet depths lay the suggestion of life in the past or future, rather than the present.

"I am growing a mere dreamer," he said again to himself one night, when this mood had been strong upon him; "what has become of all my theories? I held that happiness was not the end of existence, that it was incomprehensible any man could retain egotism, while he recognised the infinite greatness of the universe, and the countless number of the stars—that the sweet dream of love though the supreme passion of life, was not all—that duty lay not in thought but in action; and that no power short of death could bind the resistless strength of an unyielding will. It was all true; and yet when I look at that face I forget everything else, and be my surroundings what they may, the thought of her seems part of me, like my heart, animating my blood, and making the name of *Alice* throb through every pulse."

Musing in this fashion, he was pacing up and down the room, when his reflections were disturbed by a tap at the door, followed by the landlady's servant, with a message to the effect, that his watch which had been sent to be cleaned, had just arrived from the jeweller's.

" Who has brought it," he asked, " the messenger ? "

" No sir, Mrs. Raynor herself."

" Ask her in then, if you please—I have something else to give her."

As Sydney unlocked his desk to take from it a

ring which he wanted reset, the jeweller's wife entered the room; and explained in a very pleasant voice, that she brought the watch herself, because the assistant was ill, her husband engaged at the shop, and the messenger occupied at the other end of London. Her manner was quiet and self-possessed, but chancing to glance towards the other end of the room, she faltered, and greatly to Sydney's surprise left the sentence she was uttering unfinished. Following the direction of her eyes, he observed that they rested upon Alice's portrait, with a look half of pleasure, and half of sadness; but all of recognition.

"You have seen that picture before," he said quickly.

"No sir—never before to-night. I beg your pardon — you were just telling me about this ring."

"Never mind the ring—you know something, and I want you to tell me what it is. You looked at that picture as if you recognised it; yet you say you have never seen it before. Have you seen the original?"

"Yes sir—Mrs. Fenwood has been very kind to

me—I wear this ring which she gave me as a continual reminder of her goodness."

"May I ask you how and when you came to know her?"

Mrs. Raynor hesitated.

"I am not at liberty to speak on that subject," she said, "it would pain me to do so; and might seem like a violation of confidence, besides it would do no good."

"I am actuated by no impertinent curiosity," he returned, "and have no wish to intrude on any matters in which I am not personally concerned; but there is one question which I think you can and will answer me—do you know where she is now?"

"Yes sir."

"Will you tell me?"

Mrs. Raynor again hesitated.

"I have no right to ask your motive sir," she began, "but"—

"But I will tell you—I am deeply desirous of serving that lady, in any way that lies in my power. We are old friends; and I promise by all I hold sacred, that if you give me the information I ask, you shall have no cause to regret it."

"I will trust you," was the equally frank reply, "my only reason for doubt, was that already she has had too much cause to associate me with sorrow; and I have a morbid shrinking from the idea of causing her any new trouble or annoyance however slight."

She drew a pencil from her pocket, and wrote an address upon a piece of paper which Sydney handed her, saying as she did so—

"I have not seen her since my marriage, and she may not know me by my new name; but tell her that I am happier now than in the old days I ever hoped to be—that I often think gratefully of her generous forgiveness of me, when she had bitter cause to hate my name; and the gentleness with which she came to see me in my sorrow, when her own fortunes were altered—and she had nothing but brave true words to give."

"You have not yet told me the name by which she will remember you."

Mrs. Raynor looked once more at the picture, with the same expression in her face, that had been perceptible when she saw it first; then she said slowly—

"She knew me as Mary Ford."

Sydney inclined his head in acknowledgment, but did not speak: perceiving that he was in no mood for further discussion of business, Mrs. Raynor softly said " Good-night " and left him, wondering in her womanly fashion, why he should have been so moved, and weaving romances on the subject until she reached her home.

Sydney sat looking at the writing, which had so unexpectedly fallen in his hands, as an alchemist would have regarded the triumphant sequel of a life-time's hitherto unrequited toil. A single glance had sufficed to burn the eagerly sought words upon his memory; yet he treasured the paper, as though it were the clue in which lay his only hope of threading the labyrinth between himself and Alice. He hardly dared to think she was at that moment only distant a few miles from him; and would have felt it at once easier and more probable of attainment, had the way been over mountains and across seas; but a London suburb was accessible without effort; and it would be possible for him to test the accuracy of this discovery the next day.

He found it unusually difficult on the following morning to concentrate his attention on professional matters; but at length his work (ordinarily congenial, but at that moment decidedly irrelevant and irritating) was finished; and he hurried in the direction of Mr. Stafford's house. Was some new disappointment in store for him? Should he find that she had gone, or make the yet more bitter discovery that the years had robbed her of grace—of beauty, or the deeper wealth of the soul? He threw the idea from him as a suggestion of treason; but he could not so easily shake off the fear that she might have forgotten him—that the fair dream-pictures they had both loved so well, might have been effaced from her heart, by the hands of time and sorrow.

The servant who opened the door in answer to his knock, received his inquiry with a look of some surprise; for Alice had never had a visitor before, and so it had come to be recognised in the kitchen that she never would have one.

" What name sir? " said the housemaid, when she had shown him into the library; and found after lingering as long as possible, that he did not produce a card.

" Tell Mrs. Fenwood an old friend wishes to

have the pleasure of a few minutes' conversation with her—that will be enough."

The housemaid's disposition was sentimental, and as she glided from the room with this commission, her mind was agitated by numerous romantic conjectures, as to the identity of this handsome stranger; and his reasons for assuming an air of mystery.

Alice entered the room expecting to be greeted either by one of the acquaintances who had known her in her wealth, and found forgetfulness convenient at the time of her poverty, or else to be confronted by the honest sunburnt face of a Seafern fisherman; but when she saw Sydney she felt her self-control momentarily forsaking her; and the hot blood flushed her face, like the burning avowal of her secret thoughts. Sydney saw her blush and tremble, and thought this agitation had done more to cancel the years of separation, than could have been effected by any words; it only lasted for an instant however, and when he held her hand in his she was very pale.

He sat down beside her, and they talked chiefly of the less important things which had happened

since their last meeting; but Alice's manner was
constrained and nervous, and something of the
coldness which had been perceptible in her conversation at the time when Miss Gordon's
influence was strongest upon her, slightly marred
it now. As Sydney spoke and listened, he felt
that strange happiness which rises high above all
common sensations; and yet is closely akin to
sharp and pitiless pain. To be near her—to watch
not an unchanging shadow, but the sweet reality
of her beautiful face—to hear her musical voice;
and thus to connect the severed past and present,
was more than gladness; but through it all ran
an uneasy consciousness that he only seemed to
be near her—that as they talked, they were standing on the opposite banks of a river, unable to
clasp hands because the relentless stream of a long
absence flowed between. While he was thinking
of this, Alice proposed to introduce him to her
uncle and aunt; and all further possibility of
rising above conversational commonplace was at
an end.

Shortly after this, the Staffords, accompanied by
Alice, left London for the seaside, where they

stayed two months. On their return Sydney called again, but on this, as well as on two or three subsequent occasions, he did not see Alice alone, much to his annoyance, as her aunt was a somewhat indifferent substitute, and *tête-à-tête* conversation with her was sometimes the only entertainment which offered itself.

Alice seemed to avoid him, but whether from pride, indifference, or the fear of betraying feelings she wished to hide he could not tell. So the autumn and winter passed away, and once more the birds sang their choral welcome to the spring.

" Has she forgotten ? " said Sydney to himself on his return home from an evening spent at Clapham. " I don't think women remember as men do ; but she surely must retain some faint thought of feelings which were powers in old days."

And meanwhile Alice was thinking—" I am nothing to him now but a friend. He sought me out because he is noble, and knew I was poor and lonely ; but he must find little in me now of the light-hearted girl of seventeen whom he loved. It is better so—far better : my brief dream of happiness was over years ago; and I am too proud to call back the words uttered when he was poor and I was rich now that our positions are reversed. And yet it is hard to know that a great love is a lifelong discipline of pain."

CHAPTER XVIII.

"Beloved, let us love so well,
Our work shall still be better for our love,
And still our love be sweeter for our work,
And both commended, for the sake of each,
By all true workers and true lovers born."

ELIZABETH BARRETT BROWNING.

ALICE had not seen Seafern for nearly six years, and since the death of Mr. Ellis had held no correspondence with any one living there. Vague rumours of change reached her from time to time, and she saw in the papers that the scheme of carrying the railway there, which had been talked of years before, was at length an accomplished fact. But in her thoughts her native village was unaltered—the pictures of memory showed no change in the old mansion where her childhood had been passed—in the rough cottages of the kindly old fishermen or in the sandy beach where she and Percy had looked for shells. "I should see much changed," Alice said to herself; and then inconsistently thought of a hundred familiar objects as unaltered by the touch of time.

To revisit the old scenes for at least a few hours —to be thus enabled vividly to recall days whose golden beauty she had only half appreciated—to surround herself with familiar faces and unforgotten scenery, had long been a wistful dream with her; but although the railway rendered such an excursion easily practicable, she had not suffered it to become more than a dream. Perhaps she dreaded recognition, and consequent questions, that would wound like swords—perhaps some touch of pride prevented her from returning, widowed and desolate, to the place which had known her in her first youth dowried by wealth and beauty. But whatever causes contributed to her inaction, they were slowly undermined by the steadily growing desire to transform her shadowy recollections and fancies into realities; so that at length she started one bright May morning by the early train for the little village associated in her mind with all the sweetest moments of her life.

At the first glimpse of Seafern from the station platform the church spire and two or three other

familiar objects made her fancy the place unchanged; but another minute showed her that
many new buildings had been erected during her
absence, and that the streets seemed busier than
of yore. She determined, however, to visit every
spot separately, and not suffer herself to be misled
by a general impression. The station had been
built some way out of the village, not more than
two or three hundred yards distant from the place
where Seafern Hall had stood. Alice felt her
heart beat faster as she noticed this, and walked
eagerly in that direction. How often she had
thought of the old Hall, crumbling and deserted,
or tenanted by strangers! Her darkest fancy had
been that it might be pulled down, and a more
modern residence erected in its place; but she
had never encouraged this, imagining, reasonably
enough, that no one who could endure the dreamy
quiet of the fishing village would be indifferent to
the grave beauty of the ancient house.

But in a few moments she stood still, and looked
round her in hopeless bewilderment. The noble
trees, which had once spread their stately boughs
in the shadow of the old Hall, had been felled

long since, and carted away for timber—the soft
green lawn had given place to a dreary waste of
reddish-coloured earth — instead of the flowers
which had once redeemed the sombre aspect of
the place by their gay parade of blue, red, and
yellow, were outhouses, sheds, and a long row of
badly built cottages, while in place of Seafern
Hall stood a large factory, which seemed to con-
front her with a meaningless stare from each of
its curtainless windows.   As she stood regarding
the great square monstrosity, half fancying it
must be a hateful dream, the bell rang for dinner,
and a crowd of young men and girls flocked
noisily from the building.   Their faces were all
strange to her, and they spoke with an unfamiliar
provincialism : Alice looked round longingly for
something that should remind her, in however
poor a way, that this was still the Seafern she had
known ; but her quest was fruitless, and she turned
away weary and faint of heart.

In the village it was much the same—the commercial element was apparent everywhere—several
of the old shops had given way to the showier
tenements of more enterprising tradesmen, or re-

tained an existence more flourishing than of yore, by conforming to the altered spirit of the times. The little village inn, called "The Jolly Fisher-men," where the customers (to whose calling com-plimentary allusion was thus made) had formerly indulged in sober potations of ale, and told tales of storm and shipwreck through oracular fumes of tobacco, was closed; but no one noticed so insig-nificant a circumstance except Alice, who remem-bered how Datchby had once been the presiding genius of the house; for opposite this low-roofed scene of rustic conviviality was a gaudy tavern flaunting with lamps, plate glass, and bad imita-tions of granite and marble, which proclaimed in letters a foot long that its proud designation was the Station Hotel, while to complete the impressive aspect of the stately establishment there hung in the principal window a printed announcement that Mr. Griffin, the celebrated lecturer from London, would that evening address his fellow-countrymen in the adjoining hall on the wrongs of the British working man and the rapacious tyranny of the higher classes.

Some of the people glanced curiously at Alice as

she passed rapidly down the street; but her face was almost hidden by a thick veil, and no one recognised her. As she got farther away from the factory the universal alteration, though still apparent, became less striking; and she saw many faces she had known, which would she knew, have softened and brightened had they discovered who she was. But her heart ached too bitterly for that, and she hurried on.

Even the cottages of the fishermen were unlike what they had been of old, for the more profitable trades had left the fishing in the hands of a few old men in whom habit was too deeply rooted to permit a change of life. The smoke and dust were everywhere; and a beershop, recently built, destroyed the last remnant of the picturesque in the scene. Datchby's cottage was little altered; but when Alice reached the lonely little dwelling, which her mother had thought of as a fairy palace— which had so often echoed the merry sounds of her father's songs and laughter—where she herself had been born, and spent the first years of her life, all she saw seemed to mock her tender thoughts of home. Through the open door Alice saw that the small rooms were cheerless and untidy—a fact fully explained by the appearance of a hard-featured, slovenly woman, who stood there shrewishly scolding some small children playing in the little garden.

With a heavy heart Alice turned away, and walked on wearily till she reached the little church : here there were some preparations for partial restoration, but the change seemed less unkindly, and she opened the heavy iron gate of the churchyard with a feeling that at last she had reached a spot where no rough reality would slight remembrance, and scatter preconceived ideas. She lingered a little while by the grave of George Ellis, and read the simple inscription until her eyes were dim; then she passed on until she reached the grassy mound where nearly twenty years before, her father and mother had within a few days of each other been laid to rest.

Alice's character was naturally self-reliant and strong, and she was little accustomed to give way to passionate outbursts of grief, feeling generally in the hours of keenest pain the tearless misery which is hardest of all to bear. But at that

moment her self-control failed her utterly—
for the first time in her life she felt robbed at
once of memory and hope ; and kneeling by the
grassy grave, she sobbed like a terrified child ;
and the cry of her heart unconsciously shaped
itself in the words, wailed rather than spoken—

"Mother—mother—comfort me, for I am weak,
and desolate, and lonely."

As if in answer to her appeal, she felt a touch
upon her shoulder, light and tender as the
mother's whose aid she so passionately invoked ;
and in another minute strong arms had gently
raised her from the ground.   Throughout the
morning she had felt an excited misgiving that
she was merely an actress in a troubled dream ;
and now the same vague impression deprived her
of astonishment when she saw that Sydney Mayfield was standing beside her.

She tried to speak, but could not—he only said
gently, "I understand," in a tone that absolved
her from the necessity of immediate speech ; and
drawing her hand through his arm, led her from
the churchyard into the high road beyond.

For a few minutes neither of them spoke—

then Sydney talked of unimportant things, of the winding road—of a cloud's fantastic shape, of the aerial progress of a bird. Alice hardly knew if the moment was one of exquisite happiness, or cruel pain; so contrasting were the feelings in her heart. Her nerves were still quivering with the first shock of surprise and disappointment; but on the other hand, he was near her—his manner showed that she occupied the first place in his thoughts—his voice sounded as tender and musical as it had done long years ago; and she felt the luxury, so dear to a woman, yet never experienced in her life before, of complete submission to an intellect and will, known to be stronger than her own. They had walked in this way for some time, when he stopped abruptly and said, pointing to a shady path running from the main road—

" Does not that lead to Sunrise Peak ? "

She smiled assent, and answered rather sadly, " That may be altered like everything else."

" Let us go and see," he said, and in another minute they were clambering up the rough ascent. The physical exercise invigorated Alice, as the sea breezes used to do, in the far-off past—the climbing engrossed her attention too, and enabled her to recover her wonted self-possession sooner than she could otherwise have done. When they reached the summit they found no austere fulfilment of her prophecy, for everything looked as it had done when they were there together long ago.

For a little while they stood watching the sea below them in silence; then he caught both her hands in his, and said rapidly—

"Nearly eight years ago Alice darling, I said I loved you. You were little more than a child then, and I though older, was inexperienced and foolish enough. I would not wrest a promise from you, though I dared to hope you were not wholly unwilling to give it; but words are lightly spoken in life's Maytime, and I left you free. The lonely years intervening between then and now have had much of pain for us both; but the dreary time of separation is over dearest, and on this spot, which I vow to you to be holy ground since here long ago I spoke of love, and you deigned to listen, I declare that I have never been guilty of a moment's forgetfulness since then—that your fair face and true brave heart are, and have ever been, the dearest things on earth to me."

The hands he held in his trembled, but her voice did not falter as she answered quickly—

"Can you talk to me like this? You forget that I seemed to slight you in that far-off time—that now I am poor, desolate and friendless—a woman whose girlhood has passed, and whose light-heartedness has gone for ever."

"It has not gone," he answered, "for I know now that you love me, and love asks no other wealth to fill its chalice of gladness to the brim. Darling, the thought of you was with me in all my wanderings; and since my return to England my dearest companion has been a painting of your loveliness, in whose sweet meaning I have striven persistently to read some remembrance of me. Alice—more truly loved now than in the first flush of my hot-hearted youth, life can never be complete without you—I ask the highest treasure of the earth—your promise to become my wife."

Her eyes were cast on the ground, and she remained silent, contending with conflicting feelings

but when he repeated his last words, she looked
up into his face and said—

" I will not meet your noble appeal by unworthy
coquetry. If I had been less constant since our
last parting—if I had suffered for an instant new
interests to efface the memory of the words which
crowned me with the knowledge of your love, I
would not dare to accept the gift you offer now.
But I have always loved you Sydney—I loved
you before we ever met, when I had only heard of
you, and associated you in my childish fancy with
the heroes of all the fairy tales I read—I loved
you when we rowed together on that sunny sea—
when you told me your secret here where we are
standing now—when we parted, as it seemed for
ever; and throughout all the cruel aftertime that
has succeeded. I thought I had buried the sense
of happiness for ever; but since you say you love
me still, my heart is filled with a gladness almost
too great to bear."

Once before they had kissed each other, but it
had been in the pathetic retrospect of a concluded
past, and the bitterness of a farewell believed to
be eternal. Now he again clasped her in his arms

and pressed his lips to hers; but this time it was as the mute avowal of an undying constancy—of a love that should be a deep and strong reality, when the world should have disappeared like a vapour—when the light of sun, and moon, and stars should have been quenched; and the great sea, with its boundless expanse of impetuous waters should have become a forgotten thing.

THE END.